Blue
Sunflower
Startle

Blue
Sunflower
Startle

a novel

by
YASMIN LADHA

Library and Archives Canada Cataloguing in Publication

Ladha, Yasmin
      Blue sunflower startle / written by Yasmin Ladha.

ISBN 978-1-55481-016-1

      I. Title.

PS8573.A2798B58 2010   C813'.54   C2010-903890-8

Freehand Books
412 – 815 1st Street SW
Calgary, Alberta
Canada T2P 1N3
www.freehand-books.com

BOOK ORDERS
Broadview Press Inc.
280 Perry Street, Unit 5
Peterborough, Ontario
Canada K9J 7H5
Phone: 705-743-8990
Fax: 705-743-8353
customerservice@broadviewpress.com
www.broadviewpress.com

Edited by Robyn Read.
Cover design by David Drummond, <www.salamanderhill.com>.
Interior design by Eileen Eckert.

Printed on FSC recycled paper and bound in Canada.

Freehand Books, an imprint of Broadview Press Inc., acknowledges the financial support for its publishing program provided by the Government of Canada through the Canada Book Fund.

Freehand Books gratefully acknowledges the support of the Canada Council for the Arts for its publishing program.

 Canada Council **Conseil des Arts**
for the Arts **du Canada**

For Salim

Contents

The Entrance

Savoury Orange Duck in a Stompy Orange Home   11

At the Back of My Skull   20

Coca-Cola and Cowboys   30

Before Allah Troubles You, First He Will Seek Your

    Permission   46

That Mama Has Big Buttocks   59

Another Journey, Another Reincarnation   68

The Exits

Departing   83

Almost Bridal   87

Connecting   97

Away From Home, An Upright Place   101

Boarding   119

Speak Gor Gor Sweet   123

Arriving   153

Acknowledgements   165

About the Author   167

The Entrance:

1964–1976

Tukuyu
Dodoma
Dar es Salaam

Tanzania, East Africa

Savoury Orange Duck in a Stompy Orange Home

The town of Dodoma is in the heart of Tanzania, like a nose, plop centre in the middle of a face. Our grandparents have a flourmill in Dodoma. Mother has taught us their address:

P. O. Box 11

Dodoma

Tanzania.

She is making my brother and I practice their telephone number, #9.

We live in Tukuyu, in the southern highlands of Tanzania. Mount Rungwe rises in the distance. We can see it from the sitting room. In its belly lives a monkey with thick brown fur. Its calling, scabrous, like a car horn fused with a dog's bark. It puffs out cold air that mists Tukuyu mornings.

Mother serves us tea biscuits at 4 p.m.

"Cry short, will you not, my dear?" she asks of me. I stop straightaway. I am a good girl.

Once I saw a woman, pretty as a nurse, inside the moon. She was smiling down at me. I screamed and screamed. That time, I did not cry short. Mother said I was still good.

Dodoma is far away from Tukuyu, almost two days by car. The first stop is Mbeya, where passengers halt for a treat of canned fish sandwiches and milky coffee. Canned food, like apples wrapped in crinkly paper, is dear, reserved for trips and special occasions. After Mbeya, an overnight stay in Iringa, and finally, Dodoma. From wet green grasses of Tukuyu to thorny trees. Crowded stars hammer Dodoma's desert sky. The moon is a witch doctor's murky orange, like an egg gone bad.

Grandmother has visited us in Tukuyu, each time carrying her maroon bread-shaped purse. Last visit (Grandfather has never joined her) she took me on a bus trip to Mbeya to visit Grandfather's relatives. She is dutiful in carrying out Grandfather's obligations.

"Isn't Mbeya green as Scotland?" she asked, pointing to the misty hills. Neither of us had visited Scotland. I pictured Father's Land Rover gliding over the hills covered with slippery grasses tall as the Masai who drink blood and milk mixed together and do not wear underwear.

I told Grandmother that my brother, who was born in Mbeya at the missionary hospital, could spot Father's Land Rover anywhere, and he was just two. Before we arrived at the Mbeya bus depot, Grandmother lifted me off the seat to catch me in a calliper's vice between her haunches. I raised my arms so she could change my frock. Then she sat me down again facing the window and combed my hair in fierce strokes. I was almost five. This was 1963. Even Father did not know he was sick. Mother wore red high-heeled shoes with gold straps to parties.

Now I am almost six. Father is too weak to come downstairs to open the store. He lies in bed in his green robe. Mother still dabs Apple Blossom scent behind her ears, but her face has gone away.

For days, Mother makes us hot cocoa with froth on top. We drink in the sitting room, like guests, and take turns with Mr. View Finder. We have plenty of slides. There is a slide of the moustached green tinkerbird; Mount Rungwe's natural bridge called the Bridge of God; a grand Mombasa ship; another one of a giant, unsmiling guard in red headgear who stares right into your eyes; and a powdery woman, Marilyn Monroe, her face ready to kiss you. Mother tells me to look after my little brother before she shuts her and my father's bedroom door. She and Father whisper in there for hours.

Then, one day, my brother and I wave Mother and Father good-bye from a white car. A stranger-uncle is driving us to Dodoma where we will stay with our grandparents. We watch Mother and Father through the rear window of the white car: they stand on the steps of our general store, Mother's arm firmly around Father's waist. Soon they will leave for Nairobi where Father will be admitted to a big hospital. You have to pass Masai land close to Arusha-with-red-soil to reach Nairobi in Kenya, another country. Silently I recite what will be our new address like Allah's name:

P.O. Box 11
Dodoma
Tanzania
Telephone #9.

I hope that the memorization cools Mother's liver, knowing that we will not get lost. From Mother, we already know that our grandparents' house has the shape of a horseshoe, starting with Grandfather's office, followed by many, many rooms, and that it ends with the mill on the other side.

It is 1964. We are leaving Tukuyu in Stranger-Uncle's car, Mount Rungwe rising above the town.

At the back of the car, we swerve from one door to another.

"This is a Peugeot," my brother whispers.

Stranger-Uncle shoots over the potholes, yelling, "Children, sing if you wish!" Both Brother and I are on tip-top behaviour. When it gets dark, we suck our thumbs. My brother makes me smell his stinky thumb. I readily do. I am his mother now, his right-hand angel. We do not stop in Mbeya for canned fish sandwiches, and when we do not spend a night in a hotel in Iringa, my brother and I plough punches into each other's stomachs, but quietly, so Stranger-Uncle will not know.

At our grandparents' home, half the men are to the right, half to the left of the huge entrance door, pulling it open.

"A Mombasa ship could pass through," my brother whispers. I bend low to hear him.

As the mill workers pull the door open, the knots in their calves bunch up.

The Mombasa-ship door is only fully split open on special occasions: Eid or when grain is transported upcountry and empty lorries back slowly through the door, ready to be filled with gunny sacks of wheat and rice. The Mombasa-ship door has a small door built in it for everyday use. The mill has a different entrance entirely for customers, two public doors that open into the street. Customers enter through these doors with baskets of grains to be ground into flour. Then, like a box within a box, there is a long rectangular room with a low ceiling inside the mill, cosy as a kangaroo's pocket. My brother and I christen this room, quiet as a cave, the Belly Room.

The Belly Room has doors that open directly into a veranda. This veranda, in between, connecting mill to house, is wide as a field. One end of the veranda is close to the dining room, has a washbasin, and an outside sitting room. The other end of the veranda ends with the mammoth entrance door.

Grandmother's Singer sewing machine is in the outside sitting room. The room has bulky chairs but no coffee table. Teacups are placed out of harm's way by the sides of chairs. There is Grandfather's rose bin, where a mild snake lives. And there is the well, which has been filled with dirt for a long time because once a drunken mill worker fell into it. Now, Grandmother grows herbs and vegetables on top. Only its circular wall gives away that it was once a well.

Generally, Grandfather conducts business in the outside sitting room, which bustles with activity and aromas of cooking, the scuttle of people and chickens. Strangers and people Grandfather does not care for are directed to the Dead Office, a room hardly used. Dogs prefer to die in the quiet and dark of this room. Compared to the rest of the house, its location is distant, away from the hustle—it is the first room to the right of the mammoth door.

After the Dead Office, the bedrooms follow. The last bedroom is Grandmother's. It is Grandfather's as well. His possessions everywhere: a basket of newspapers, slippers by his ottoman, Brylcreem, a pocket comb he uses, a gold-trimmed brush-and-comb set he never uses, and his packet of skinny Ten Cent cigarettes on his bedside table with a wooden knob. When Grandfather turns the knob clockwise, out comes a nifty hoop for his water glass.

Grandfather will come to say to us, "Fetch me a pillow from your Grandmother's room."

"Isn't it yours as well?" Brother and I will ask.

"Of course! But your grandmother is my liver." He means he loves her very much.

There is a shamba of mango and jamun trees underneath Grandparents' bedroom window. An oily, haphazard hedge surrounds the shamba. Beady, cankerous flowers glower on the ground. Their thorns, dainty as fish bones, look like they could draw blood. Directly under the window are little mounds of jasmine beds, gentle as babies' graves. Grandmother does not touch the jasmines, she tells us, and she does not want us walking into the shamba in the evenings when spirits come out to stretch their legs. Come the call to prayers in the evening, I know I will not let Brother out of sight.

Last, there is the inside sitting room. It has a black piano that no one plays. Grandfather bought it from an English woman returning home after Tanzania's independence. No one buffs it, I notice. In Indian films, pianos shimmer.

The mill grinds corn, millet, and nutty wheat flour for rotis.

"A miller grinds flour. A baker bakes bread," my brother, Mr. Pompous Panjandrum, tells me. But when Mother told us about the mill, I had imagined a welcome spread of round cakes with jam in the middle and fondant icing on top.

"Round iced cakes are baked in their huge horseshoe house," I had boasted to my brother in Tukuyu.

Seeing my crestfallen face the day we arrive, Grandmother storms into Mzee Mamudu's kitchen. Mzee Mamudu has been with our grandparents for years, even before Mother got married. He is next in command of the household after Grandmother. Grandmother spends a quick hour in his kitchen making a duck out of mashed potatoes.

"The closest thing I know to baking," she apologizes, setting the duck on an oval serving plate with blue windmills. The duck has Black Cat bubble gum eyes. Grandmother used the back of her eyebrow pencil to notch out the eye sockets. Her palms are stained yellow from the wet saffron worms she dangled on the duck's beak.

I miss Mother. Mother is not tiny. She is heavy like Grandfather.

"My daughter after all!" Grandfather likes to say, full of pride.

Mother smells of Apple Blossom scent. Her hair has puffy waves like Mzee Mamudu's chapattis. She wears it loose.

When Mother phones first time, I do not ask why she did not tell us about the entrance door, that not a dinghy, but a ship could get through it. How could she have forgotten?

Then, on the fortnightly telephone calls to Mother at the Nairobi cancer hospital, Mother's voice, like her face, goes away. I warn my brother that good children do not ask questions—but I break my own rule, on the phone, when I ask her, "Is Father still in his robe?"

Her answer will tell me when we will be together again. The day he comes down for breakfast dressed, we will return to Tukuyu.

In the Belly Room, sacks of wheat and maize wait to be lorried to different places in town and upcountry. Engines revving, the trucks wait to be loaded. No one names the cats trailing up and down the Belly Room. They prefer to deliver their kittens here, high up on gunny sacks, against the hum of the mill. Drivers ignore last minute advice from Mzee Mamudu to go pole-pole, gently. It is like in one ear, out the other. Our bare feet register the trembling ground of the cemented veranda.

"Like an earthquake," my brother says. His hair is bleached from Dodoma's desert sun. He is already the king of the street, riding the red bicycle Grandfather bought him. At night, he sleeps with me. We both suck our thumbs like a dirty secret.

Hush.

The Belly Room holds silent baskets of flour, each covered with a white cloth. Our grandparents will personally deliver them to the women of the town. I already know Jena Bai's has a red rim. She is a spinster old as Grandmother. Grandfather has adopted her as his sister. Mama Titi's basket is of the palest straw. Mama Titi has huge breasts. The senior boys at the Aga Khan Secondary School nickname her breasts Mount Kilimanjaro and Mount Kenya. Mama Titi jokes, "Call them K. K. Alps, short and light." Rabia Bai gets two baskets, maybe because she delivers babies, I do not ask. My new home has unspoken rules. Certain things are not meant to come to the lips, like mention of Father's cancer. When the big door is opened and half the town witnesses the activity of the veranda, Grandmother's face grows pale with a sober wariness.

Men will be at work, children at school. Only then, Grandfather and Grandmother knock on the women's doors.

Knock, knock, but never together.

In matters of charity, our grandparents do not share a collarbone allegiance. Grandfather says that in this matter, the right hand need not know what the left hand is doing. Their lists are private as fasts.

In the Belly Room stacked with gunny sacks and baskets of grain we have bees. Not ship-shape ones making honey. Heady from flour, our bees are on wobbly flights, like Grandfather smitten with Allah.

"A worshipper may fast or lick water off a leaf. Who is to know? That's between Allah and His servant, nobody else's business," Grandfather reminds us, my brother on one of his knees and me on the other, the nourishing pemmican of his words strengthening our bones, rocking us to Allah. "To keep fast is an unrehearsed whisper in Allah's ear. You pester Him. You adore Him. You tulip turban Him to you, chat with Him out of a hungry mouth, or cheat Him. That is your business with the Almighty, so meddling mullahs better step aside!"

"Or take a restful trip to Dodoma Mental Hospital!" adds my brother, saucily copying Grandfather. When Indians balk at his frivolity with Allah (like, how dare he think of Allah as a pretty maiden pouring his wine?), not to mention his shoulder-rubbing with the Africans, he tells them, right to their faces, "Take a restful trip to Dodoma Mental Hospital!"

Only after Brother's echo does Grandmother intervene. "Steady, my heart. Speak gor gor sweet. Why involve the children?" Grandmother is careful of Allah and of the people in Dodoma. She wears a sensible black watch, its exquisite Swiss precision sensibly hidden.

When Grandfather gets up to make himself a drink, Grandmother smoothes his cushion to straighten the upheaval he has created.

But Grandfather is mighty heavy, and even when bathing, late afternoons, he lustily sings Allah's praises. When he comes out of the bathroom, there are blots of pink prayers on his skin scrubbed with Lifebuoy. With a gleam in his eye, he kicks doors open like a cowboy. I am only six years old, but even I know the town watches his beefy gait.

Besides Allah, Grandfather is smitten with Tanzania as well, formerly Tanganyika, made independent from the British the same year my brother was born, in 1961. Julius Kambarage Nyerere is our President, the first president of Tanzania. Before he became President he was a teacher, so we call him Mwalimu, teacher in Swahili. Swahili is now the national language of Tanzania.

When he first took office, Grandfather admired our young President, educated British but African in decorum. He met Mwalimu Nyerere right after independence, when Mwalimu wanted to meet influential dukawallahs—that is, the shopkeepers in small towns. Mwalimu placed his left hand under his right elbow, only then shook Grandfather's hand.

"Shikamoo, Mzee," Mwalimu Nyerere greeted Grandfather.

Because Grandfather was much older, Mwalimu called him Mzee, elder wise man. Grandfather likes to tell the story standing up. When he pivots he does it trimly, sure of the ground beneath.

"I was all shook up," he tells us.

Once Grandfather gets going, whisky breath or not, there is no stopping him. "We Indians *are* the mercantile adventurers. What can we not do for this country?"

Then Grandmother, if she is around, tugs his hand gently, says, "The wind rises of its own accord. Don't tip the dhow willy-nilly, my love," she cautions. She, like the others, already smells the hunt.

She is mindful.

Grandfather is besotted with Allah and Tanzania.

And he has enemies.

Before we put on our underwear, my brother and I shake them to check for nestling cockroaches and bees.

Grandmother instructs us, "Do the triple-check, as if you are crossing Main Street."

Daily, my brother rides his red bicycle up and down the street. I am on the lookout for him.

When he loses his tooth, I put a shilling under his pillow.

My brother and I are inside a protective circle.

Orange is the colour of our new home.

At the Back of My Skull

Dodoma Hotel is opposite the Dodoma railway station. Uncle Chando, the manager of the Hotel, is from the Chagga tribe in Moshi where the snow-capped Kilimanjaro rises in their backyards. He makes the best sherry trifle. White plates arrive with a flourish. A waiter wearing white gloves swings the plate in a Frisbee arc, only to lay it soundlessly in front of the diner. The plates are delightfully, weirdly warm. Every Eid, Uncle Chando arrives at my grandparents' with two bowls of sherry trifle, compliments of Dodoma Hotel. He has a tribal mark between his eyebrows the size of a shilling. He taught Grandfather to brew mbege from Chaggaland, made of millet and bananas and left to ferment for ten days. Now, every Christmas, Uncle Chando comes over for Grandfather's mbege.

The railway station and the Dodoma Hotel are in the European section of town, which also has the post office, swimming pool, and the Dodoma Mental Hospital. European missionaries in pastel dresses (with shirt collars), their hankies tucked in their buckram belts, are the only European women who ride pikipikis in Dodoma. The rest of the European ladies drive cars. But one Indian woman drives. She is tall as the Europeans, and, like them, wears her hair short and shops at Household and Sundries on Main Street. She is from Nairobi, the London of East Africa, and married into the wealthiest family in Dodoma. They are the only Indians who live in the European section, and they live in a sprawling, flamingo-pink mansion. Though her husband has invested in a winery (the first in Tanzania), owns the Dodoma bus depot (soon to be nationalized), the Dodoma sports club (soon to be nationalized) that has a statue of a giant whisky bottle on its front lawn, and the only bicycle shop in town, folks still wonder why the daughter of an established coffee planter chose to marry and settle in this dusty town. Although both her sons were born in Dodoma, the town keeps its distance from Tall Woman, not out of small town snobbery but because she spooks them. They think she can do Ganga magic.

Grandparents live in the middle of town along with other Indian merchants. The tower of our jamatkhana is the first landmark a visitor from the railway station spots, while a short distance away a grey cathedral on a spread of emerald green lawn marks the beginning of the European section. Though both the Sikh gurdwara and the Hindu temple are located in the middle of town, they are ordinary houses converted into worship houses, without plush gardens, domes, or tower clocks.

In between the European and Indian sections of town is Main Street, with Ramson's Cinema, Barclays Bank, and Household and Sundries which stocks imported products galore: canned fruit salad, dried figs, orange squash, crackers, canned herring in tomato sauce, sugared rice puffs, cornflakes, apples in tissues, and whisky in dimpled bottles. Its other section sells Japanese silk, ribbons, wedding lace, buttons, and German knives, coveted for their craftsmanship.

Then, there is the busy African section, almost at the end of town and just past the sokoni where vegetables, fruit, and live chickens are sold; where, in a big, white-tiled room, butchers wait to take orders behind a bloody counter they keep wiping down with a wet rag. Past the sokoni, there is the mosque and houses that are almost stuck to one another, the lanes as narrow as the lanes of Arabic suqs, winding this way and that. Mama Titi lives here. She sells her coveted dried fish and beef behind her house. Henna that brings the ripest maroon-brown to hands and feet is sold in the African section, along with frankincense from Salalah and myrrh from Mecca. And when you want Ganga magic done on someone, you come here as well.

Behind the sokoni, Indian shopkeepers have African tailors bent over sewing machines. They pedal away in bright rubber slippers outside the shops littered with wormy threads—you would think no one laid a broom there. Close by, the tea seller's cart is under a shady mango tree. Folks stop for chai and news after their market purchases. Lorries honk, cyclists get out of the way, dogs copulate, the Aga Khan Primary School's second bell of the day rings out from the Indian section, at recess, ten sharp, just as the pong of garbage ripens. It is a bustling morning in Dodoma.

Household and Sundries on Main Street remains bright with silence. Its mopped floors sparkle. The exotic fragrance of apples (each wrapped in a crinkly tissue) suffuses the store. Royal whisky bottles are cushioned in purple silk. The only zebra crossing in town is off the steps of Household and Sundries, and Barclays Bank is right next door.

And then there is our droning mill.

The portly bees.

I carry Father and Mother under the bump where the skull dents and slides down to become friendly with my nape, my place of secrets. Grandmother gathers my hair in a thick bundle at that very spot. For sneaky hairs, she slides the comb sideways until she has got them all. My head swishes with refreshed blood. Grandmother sprints a swift plait down my back. The back of my skull screwed on, tight. Where is my little brother? I cannot spot his red bicycle.

One day, Brother gulps down red wine. Grandfather had left the bottle by his chair in the outside sitting room. Brother totters about until Mzee Mamudu comes to his rescue. The household is in a frenzy. Grandmother has apples rushed from Household and Sundries. Grandfather speeds off in his green Peugeot to the chemist's shop to buy him a red toy sports car. (The chemist's is the only toyshop in Dodoma.)

After returning from the shop, Grandfather tucks my brother, dead with sleep, behind him in the wide bed he shares with Grandmother. Usually when Grandfather naps he tucks a cool pillow between his legs, and Grandmother's tiny form radiates beside him. But this entire day, Grandmother will have nothing to do with her husband.

"As if there isn't enough happening in their lives already," Grandmother says, shrugging off Grandfather's pleas. She goes about her business, not once calling him, "my love."

I stay with my brother as well, sitting up at the other end of the bed. The almari is not fully closed. Grandfather must have left it open when he pulled on his itchy London pants before he rushed off to the chemist's. When Grandmother is mad with him, Grandfather puts on his itchy London pants to please her. Heavy wooden hangers are for these pants that Grandmother imports from Gentlemen's Court on Bond Street. Grandfather's pants and jackets, whether starched or dry cleaned, hang upright on hangers.

"Your grandfather's clothes are on guard. He's the front room, I'm the back room," Grandmother teaches me.

However, Grandfather most often wears thin drawstring cotton pyjamas in the mill. This gets Grandmother's goat. She asks him, is he a coolie or a boss? Only then Grandfather pulls on the cotton slacks he wears in the evenings to Dodoma Hotel for his regular double peg of Chivas. But as for the itchy pants, Grandfather says it makes perfect sense to wear woollen suits for his visits to Tukuyu. Although he never visited us. I ease his lie with a smile, like Grandmother smoothing his cushions when he gets up in a huff or to freshen his drink.

In the cupboard, Grandmother's silk bundles are on shadowed shelves beneath Grandfather's neatly hung clothes. At home, men get precedence in a cupboard. Grandmother only wears ankle-length dresses. She piles them on large squares of silk. She ties the opposite corners of the squares together. Three knots on top.

"The middle knot," she tells me, "is the middle eye of Lord Shiva that protects the people of the house."

Grandmother sews my dresses in secret, so that it is a surprise for me. Many times when I lift my pillow at bedtime, I find a new dress, pressed and folded in a tidy square. Now, when I shake open a cloth serviette in a restaurant, I half expect it will unravel into a frock.

Each time my intoxicated brother sits up in bed, his red eyes scurry to find me. Satisfied, he falls into another bout of toddy sleep. I saw him first time when Mother brought him home from the missionary hospital in Mbeya. I saw him under a mosquito net that was taut as an open umbrella.

In Grandparents' bed, my brother's toes look insect-engorged. When a bee stings me, I pull out the thorn without clamour, my face grim as an adult's. Bees attack the soles of my feet. Once I remove the thorn, I hobble to the kitchen where either Mzee Mamudu or Grandmother gives me a slice of lemon to rub over the buckram-hard swelling. The day I do this and wash my hair all by myself, I will be considered old enough to be left alone. I soothe my brother's feet with ice wrapped in a tea towel and munch on the costly apples our grandparents bought for him.

When my brother gets over his hangover, right away he asks for a yellow crane truck to go with his new red sports car.

The cosy door that opens into the Belly Room gets the attention of dust that once swept off your doorstep is not yours anymore, even if it whooshes right back, dancing around your ankles. This door gets a fresh coat of vanilla paint before every Eid. Grandmother fasts the whole thirty days and then, on Eid, the house brims with indulgences: the clang of shillings for the children of the town, new handkerchiefs for the mill workers and guests, the fragrance of frankincense, and the sweet waft of saffron milk and pink sherbet that Mzee Mamudu prepares. Forgotten under the washbasin are toppled white bowls stained with henna from the night before.

The night before Eid, we wait for the moon. Though it is close to two years that my brother and I have been living in Dodoma, it is our first Eid with our grandparents; we did not celebrate last Eid in Tukuyu because Father was sick, and our parents sent us to Dodoma after the Eid holiday. Will the moon come out tonight?

Then at last, when the moon slowly ekes out a blurry shape, Grandmother cakes our palms with shivery henna. We make fists, and she wraps bandages around our hands; they bleed orange through the bandages. My brother and I are invalids, hand-fed scrumptious treats.

Early the next morning, the roar of the gargantuan entrance door opening wakes us. Lorries are reversing into the veranda to be loaded up. In crystal glasses, Mzee Mamudu ladles out sherbet with glistening black things my brother calls frogs' eggs. We have bright orange-brown palms by breakfast, the morning of Eid. Today, we will wear new clothes and new Bata shoes.

Every month, a witch doctor arrives to sprinkle a trail of powder like termite poison, followed by a mullah who recites verses from the Quran. When they leave, Grandmother gives them each a rooster, four shillings, and a wraparound cloth. Mzee Mamudu tells us the wraparound is the only underwear they wear. My brother and I do not believe him. What if the sheet comes undone?

Mzee Mamudu says, "Then the wearer's face will be red as a monkey's ass."

My brother and Mzee Mamudu laugh. Both agree Africans should wear proper underwear, it is about time, and that includes the Masai. But for the Masai, European underwear would be as devastating as leaving home. Has my brother forgotten he knows what that is like? He still sucks his thumb at night.

Grandmother leaves chores to Mzee Mamudu, but polishes the five-foot tree trunk table on Kit Kat legs in the inside sitting room herself. Mzee Mamudu does not mind. Mzee Mamudu tells me on his kitchen steps, "It gives Mama peace of mind. Your uncle made it for her. She was his only mother then."

The top of the table has natural swirls of circling knuckles. The two ends taper into fingernail ovals. Although Grandmother is his real mother, Uncle also has a Masai mother. Mzee Mamudu says that Uncle has stung Grandmother so bad the thorn is still in her flesh. He wants us to be out of her way. That is why he told me the secret.

"You know where Masai country is?" Mzee Mamudu asks me.

"Near Arusha, close to Nairobi."

"The Masai are crazy! Who smears shit on their bodies?"

"Mzee, it is cow dung mixed with the earth."

"Still shit. And do not forget the Masai stole your uncle from your grandmother! Before you were born, your uncle got lost in

Masai territory near Arusha. His car overturned in a mudslide after the long rains. A Masai woman nurtured him back to health, feeding him their staple of cow's blood with fresh milk, no matter how many times he retched. That was your grandmother's first death when her son could not be found."

I know the second death is when he returns.

Now, Father's cancer. On top, Grandfather's drumbeating politics, rumbling and rocking the thin calm.

"Three months later, when everyone took him for dead, your uncle returned. First thing he told your grandmother was, 'I have two mothers now,' as cruelly as declaring, 'I have two wives.'"

When he is in Dodoma, Uncle keeps to the mill and his room. He wears black-framed glasses. He goes to bed early. One day I find a magazine on his bookshelf with pictures of a naked black woman. Her yams are not like Mama Titi's. They are swollen with a spiny line between. Her private part glitters with gold sprinkles. But what shocks me most is her hair. It is not woolly but Indian straight and yellow. If she dared saunter down Main Street with such hair, people would cackle with hyena laughter.

In our first two years at the mill, we hardly see Uncle. Then, like a bolt out of the blue, one day Uncle comes to the mill to meet us. He kneels, removes his red straw hat, and says, "I float like a butterfly and sting like a bee." The boxer's words.

My brother says outright, "You are bald as an egg!"

Mzee Mamudu says, "But he has teeth," because Uncle is smiling so widely.

Uncle shaved his head in protest. Muhammad Ali is no longer King of the Ring. His country took away his title because he would not fight another country like the rest of the soldiers. The King of the Ring says they have done him no wrong, so why should he fight them?

The room I like the least at Grandparents' is bleak even when it has guests.

The dark dining room follows Grandparents' bedroom. In fact, there is a door in their wall that opens into the dining room, though

I have never seen it opened. The dining room has a single prisoner's window but sits sixteen people. It has a room beside it with cupboards stacked with dishes with blue windmills that we use everyday, as well as a set of dishes with brown windmills for our Hindu guests who do not eat eggs and meat, and a gas oven Mzee Mamudu rarely uses. Next is Mzee Mamudu's kitchen where he makes his date-and-cashew cake. He lines his clay pot with newspapers and bakes the cake on top of the stove. For biryani, he lays coals both on the top and the bottom of a pot for four hours, simmering beef and rice in a meaty stock, adding bay leaves, cardamom, and saffron languidly as a bride. When my brother requests a hot plate as if he is at the Dodoma Hotel, Mzee Mamudu rebukes him, "Son, in this pish-posh heat?"

After the storage and ironing room is my favourite place in the house: the western toilet. You climb five long and large steps to get to the throne, and there is also a basin to wash your hands! Here Brother and I read strips like *Pop, Dick and Harry* and *Dennis the Menace* in comics like *The Beezer* and *The Beano*, a whack of Bazooka bubble gum in our mouths. The western toilet was installed when Father came to Dodoma first time.

Father, from Dar es Salaam, the capital (Mother met him through a friend there), was not used to squatting. Grandmother fell in love with Father right away. She as well is from Dar es Salaam. Mzee Mamudu told us that Grandmother and Father would roar in the kitchen when he attempted chapattis, his coming out droopy with several chins. Grandfather hardly mentions Father. Once I overheard him tell Grandmother, "He smoked too much, right from the start." And in the wedding pictures, Grandfather stands aside, his legs apart, separate. Mother's lips are contorted as if the sun is too strong. Father is beaming. Grandmother's upturned gaze at him, impish.

Next to the western toilet is an elevated platform with a water tap. Mzee Mamudu kills chickens here.

"In the name of Allah, the most beneficent, the most merciful," he recites, and chops off the head in one clean motion.

The cats wait.

Mzee Mamudu throws them strings and gibbets. Their gurgles swell.

When chickens are slaughtered, feathers stick to our wet feet in the western toilet. We squeal. My brother and I have forgotten to wear our rubber slippers again. Everyone uses the basin in the veranda to brush his or her teeth because there is not one in the bathroom. So around the basin hovers the clean, buttery smell of Lifebuoy, while the bathroom has an eggy pong.

After the western toilet comes the eastern toilet that everyone else uses.

And finally, the big gulp, the space whooshed up by the mill, which begins to roar at 5:30 a.m. sharp.

When a drunken mill worker fell into the well in the veranda, it was covered up. It happened even before Father and Mother got engaged. Mzee Mamudu still chuckles when he tells the story.

"First Mzee," he means Grandfather, "bandaged the worker's bleeding hands, and then boxed his ears for being an empty coconut. The poor sod did not know whether he was coming or going!"

But I wonder if Father would be amused by Mzee Mamudu's story. In Tukuyu, one time, when a crowd at the market found it hilarious that a man had slipped on a banana peel, it irked him. "Country bumpkins," he muttered, tugging my hand, leaving the scene fast. Neither would he have cared for the way Grandfather humiliated the drunken worker. Grandfather would probably have called Father a city-softie.

Grandmother grows chilies, tomatoes, coriander, spring onions, and mint on top of the well, and they glitter madly under Dodoma's sun.

It has been two years. Father and Mother are still at the Nairobi cancer hospital. I demand Coca-Cola with lunch every day. Mzee Mamudu shows me how to use a bottle opener. I place the cap on a side plate busy with windmills.

The mill roars.

The bees.

Father remains at the back of my skull.

Secrets settle on my nape, a place unfrequented by eyes.

A home harbours secrets. Father has cancer. He is dying. Not a word.

Coca-Cola and Cowboys

The Sonara, our family jeweller and Grandmother's closest friend, visits in the afternoons. This is also when Grandmother oils my hair. Coils, dumb as cow plops, stick out of the veranda sofa; because of the stupor that glazes Dodoma afternoons, this is the only time they do not get on anyone's nerves. Grandfather and my brother scurry to the cool spot, Uncle's room. Uncle has gone to visit his Masai mother. Upon waking up from naps, everyone's mouths reek of cumin and onions. And the hair—hair wakes up hairier. Grandmother says, "For sure, here, protein cooks in the afternoons." Curly, black ant protein glistens on chests and arms.

Maa places a chilled Coca-Cola that we share beside the saucer of coconut oil; Grandmother is shortened to Maa in affection. I already had my fizzy treat with lunch, but my brother and I receive treats speedier than Pinocchio's nose grows. When we drink Coca-Cola, Grandmother and I take swigs from the bottle, cowboy style. Things are riding close. I see Father clearly, as if he is inside Mr. View Finder, in his green robe with maroon kidney beans. Is Mother staring at her palms? Has her face gone away?

In Tukuyu, when Father and Mother kept whispering in their bedroom for long mornings, my brother and I, bored with slides, would return Mr. View Finder to the toy box. We then tried on Mother's red high-heeled shoes, or watched the mist outside the sitting room window forming purple ribbons. The monkey's doing. We stared hard at Mount Rungwe, ears alert to hear the monkey's honk-bark. The mist stayed until mid-morning. Sometimes Mother forgot to heat our milk. Once, by mistake, she squirted hair-removing cream on Father's toothbrush. Father was not angry. Mother told me I was a good girl, my brother's right-shoulder angel.

When the Sonara visits Grandmother, when it is too hot to do much else except take sweaty naps and Grandmother has only supper supervision on her hands, she takes the Sonara to her bedroom, closed to Grandfather and Brother. But I am permitted entry.

Grandmother inspects the Sonara's new designs. She sighs over a necklace, or sometimes the Sonara does. Both are fond of clucking their tongues. After Mzee Mamudu returns from his siesta in the shamba, he brings them milky tea, followed by bowls of mangoes and pulpy jamuns. The Sonara prefers the berries soaked in salted water. He pops one in his mouth, resists as long as he can, rolling it about, draining off the salt. When the Sonara's mouth puckers with pleasure, I know his teeth have serrated tart flesh. The ruptured fruit purples his gums as if Mama Zu-zu has poisoned him.

"Ah jamuns," he says, "dark and sweet like Krishna the bewitcher." The Sonara is a worshipper of Lord Krishna.

If he can help it, the Sonara, a Hindu, won't touch our cooked dishes. We are Muslims, meat eaters. Quite often, Mzee Mamudu fetches snacks from the Maharajah Hotel, whose cook is a Brahmin, so there is no question of the Sonara being polluted by our cooked food—even though pots and dishes for our Hindu guests are kept separate.

While Mzee Mamudu is arranging the afternoon snack on a platter, a politician on the radio pokes fun at Indians. He says that if one Indian eats fish, the other does not, or if one Indian washes his ass with his right hand, another chooses his left. Mzee Mamudu smirks.

Untrue! No one eats with their toilet hand, neither Indians nor Africans! Mzee Mamudu is a quisling, a traitor, laughing at our expense.

The politician, now rah-rah on the topic, goes on. "A bunch of them Indians shun underground vegetables, like it is monkey meat."

"Only backward Amazon tribes eat monkeys!" I retort.

Mzee Mamudu ignores me. He bends his ear close to the radio, his scrawny bum sticking out.

When the politician says, "Nephew, do not forget eggs. Eggs for Indians is out of the question," Mzee Mamudu grins.

I say, "So now you're the lunatic's nephew? And we eat eggs, you know that!"

"Thank God for that!"

"Why does he say all Indians? We are Indians and we eat everything."

On plates with brown windmills, Mzee Mamudu sets syrupy orange jalebis and slivers of raw green papaya sautéed in light garlic and mustard seeds for the Sonara.

I say, "So, you like to hear rotten things about us and then bring us tea?"

He grins and continues to arrange my favourite on an oval platter, savoury lentil balls swished in chickpea batter and fried golden. He stuffs one in my mouth, already dipped in tamarind water.

I chew slowly. When I finish, I ask, "Do you really like that joker on the radio?"

"Who?" he asks, trying to get my goat.

"This one on the radio calling us mosquitoes."

"That bloodsucker?" Mzee Mamudu thinks he is funny.

"That lunatic."

"Are you jealous?" he asks.

"I am not going to marry *you*, so your liking him is no skin off my nose."

"But I do like the lunatic."

His directness makes push my shoulders back, harder. "Grandmother says the wind is blowing in a different direction nowadays."

Mzee Mamudu looks me in the eye, "She is right, my sweet," he says.

I say defiantly, "You do not like Indians. You do not like our family anymore. You are like Uncle who loves his Masai mother best because she is black."

"That Uncle of yours is an ass, and you, you have a coconut for a brain!" But Mzee is smiling, his thumb rubbing my nape.

Mzee Mamudu is back, familiar as armpit warmth. But during those moments when he is actually listening to what the politicians on the radio are saying, his conduct is flagrant, cruel as a mob's at a football stadium.

Last week, even in front of Grandmother, Mzee Mamudu did not turn off the radio. He continued to listen to Motor Mouth's witticisms about Indians.

One of them asked, "Have you seen a poor Indian's rickety stomach?" The black crowd shrieked. Everyone knew that bellies of Indian shopkeepers are swollen with hoard. Then the Jerry Lewis on the radio mimicked a roly-poly Indian housewife grunting. More shrieks.

"My nephews, she is so fat, she cannot bend to touch her hairy, silver-ringed toes. And brothers, her thin mosquito voice in your ear, buzzing commands, 'Up! Down! Harder! Softer! Front! Back!'"

Grandmother continued slicing the lemons. Mzee Mamudu nudged her to leave.

"People are stupid," he told her.

"Then why don't you turn the damn thing off?" she snapped back.

Mzee Mamudu hung his head down out of respect for her.

Grandmother pulled at Mzee Mamudu's hands, like she was doing a school inspection, her nose in his palms.

"I smell cumin … and Lifebuoy soap … and power." She looked up. "This is your kitchen and, irretrievably, this is your country. When will my husband understand this?"

"Mama," he said, shaking his head helplessly, "Mama."

"Africa is now for the Africans. You carry on. Listen to what you like," she said, and she left.

Grandmother's gold necklaces are thick filigree, nothing eyelash-thin. Each gold jewel from the Sonara is wrapped in fuchsia. "Spiky colour," I say, twisting the Sonara's fuchsia paper on my left index ring, a poisonous colour. "Like Mama Zu-zu's brew."

"Mama Zu-zu may be hollow in the head, but she is no witch." Grandmother says. She knows what it is like to be feared and hated. The town has been at Grandfather's throat for a long time.

Mama Zu-zu lives on the edge of town. Our mill workers live there as well, past the Peace Flats, where poor Indians live and grow voluptuous roses in their pinched-mouth gardens. Mama Zu-zu terrorizes the women and children of the Peace Flats, staring into their bedroom windows during the afternoons when the men have left for their shops after a burly sleep.

"Then why does Mama Zu-zu brush her left palm over her left eye and flick her tongue like a viper?" I tease.

"Only Allah knows," Maa says quietly. She leaves Allah alone.

"On his evening rounds, Mzee Mamudu sees ghosts in the shamba."

"You keep away from under the fruit trees at Maghrib, you hear? Not our time to be out when we are summoned to evening prayer," Grandmother tells me.

Continuing to twist the crinkly jewellery paper, I ask, "Why does the Sonara wrap the gold up in paper the size of a quartered handkerchief?"

"Because certain matters, like fasts, are not to be hullabalooed from rooftops. Like Grandfather says, your right hand need not know what your left hand is giving."

I whisper, "He does not hullabaloo about his baskets to Jena Bai and Mama Titi."

"I wish he were as discreet elsewhere." When Grandfather is effusive about Allah, Grandmother says, "He lives it up like a viceroy." She does not mean that Grandfather sits on a throne in a white suit to watch a parade. She means he *is* the parade, with his pirouetting from room to room singing, "Allah is my beloved."

Another contumacious leader for Grandmother, another boat rocker, will be Canada's Mr. Trudeau. She will get in a tizzy over Mr. Trudeau's unconventional public conduct.

"Does the Prime Minister want to scramblify things like your grandfather and bring on trouble? Look at him on TV, a self-satisfied Cheshire Cat! Have you seen any other Prime Minister pirouette behind the Queen's back or slide down the royal banister? Another hullabalooer, if you ask me."

But Trudeau will catch her eye (and mine). Not Trudeau the leader, but the sartorial dresser, a chatoyant gem in his green trench coat, red rose poking from his button hole. His style weakening our knees.

Meanwhile, for now, in dusty Dodoma where everyone is watching her husband, Grandmother wears a black leather wristwatch with gadgets cunningly concealed. She knows what she has and balances it with courtesy to others in town.

"Prudence is worth more than the sixteen pieces of bridal jewellery you bring to your husband's home," she says to me.

"I will not get married."

"Everyone does."

I will not, but no need to hullabaloo the secret at the back of my neck. I do not want to be like Mother staring at her palms. I do not want a real house. Something bad always happens.

Whereas Grandfather shows off his adoration for Allah, speaking about Him anywhere, at any time, Grandmother's submission to Allah is straight and narrow. On Wednesday evenings, Grandmother and I go to the jamatkhana. The first Du'a is at sunset.

I feel closest to Allah during Tasbih, which is sandwiched in between the two formal Arabic Du'as. Tasbih is in our Kutchi dialect.

The congregation stands up, palms upturned to heaven, expecting things to fall into them. Along with everyone else, I am fierce in my asking. This is to my Allah, not vous far, but tu close: my tu, tu, tu Allah, familiar as dal and roti. Worshippers that get the opportunity to recite the Tasbih and lead the congregation do so with earnestness, an irrevocable faith that Allah *is* listening. To each request, the congregation responds with an "Amen," guttural as a jungle drum, rising from the belly.

"Allah, lighten our burdens."

"Amen."

"Allah, ease our heartaches and sickness."

"Amen."

"Allah, grant us the resolve to carry out our good intentions."

"Amen."

"Allah, fulfill our wishes."

"Amen."

"Allah, lend everyone peace and goodness."

"Amen."

And to Him, my Allah of tu, tu, tu, I am insistent: "Give me back my father," I demand of Him.

I make sure I am standing behind Tall Woman who is from swanky Nairobi where they wear skin stockings and speak English. She brooks no scuzzy interference. Not even from Allah. She drives a turquoise car with shark fins. It hogs the road, as well as the sandy sides for pedestrians. She enters Household and Sundries wearing sunglasses, fin-shaped like her car. None of the Indians wear sunglasses, a European accessory. However, no one laughs at Tall Woman as she slowly pushes them to the top of her head, and you can clearly see how her short hair curls under her earlobes. Most women in town wear their long hair in a beehive bun, except for Tall Woman and Mrs. Bhajaj who works at Barclays Bank. Like Tall Woman she defies the rules. She sports bangs like Cleopatra. At parties, she makes an entrance in black slacks and pumps. When she does The Twist like film star Mumtaz, "Too good," everyone says. Her religion forbids the cutting of hair, but Mrs. Bhajaj has become a mod Sikh. Mr. Bhajaj is teaching her to drive. They are going to emigrate to London because Mwalimu Nyerere is changing his face. Our mill has not been taken over yet, but many Indian buildings and businesses are becoming nationalized. Mwalimu Nyerere wants Africans in top positions. Everyone knows that Indians are in trouble.

Tall Woman turns, and I catch a glimpse of her face. Her cheeks are scarred. Next to the town's women with their soft skins, her skin is nutty, suspenseful. Like Mother, when she smiles, her head is elsewhere.

One day, her younger son could not move his legs.

"Neither reason nor rhyme, the boy's legs were paralysed," Grandmother has told me. "I will say this," of Tall Woman, "her short hair did not turn grey in agony. Cool as a cucumber, that one. She was furious with Allah, and ordered Him to fix her son's legs good and proper. She instructed her son to move his foot. He did. Then, as if he already knew his mother's next instruction, slowly, the boy twitched both feet. Did she shriek for the doctor?

No! Instead, she made her son repeat the motion three more times. Only *then* she sought the doctor. I tell you that woman is another Amba."

Stories that steady Grandmother are from the *Ramayana* and the *Mahabharata*. It satisfies Grandmother to pluck examples from the Hindu epics.

In the *Mahabharata,* when Prince Bhisma refuses to marry Amba, she tells him to take a good look at her because he is staring at his own death. I want to be like Tall Woman, another Amba, who will not take no for an answer.

Most folk keep out of her way like she is another Mama Zu-zu. But in the jamatkhana, I'm right behind her, wanting any drizzle from her to precipitate on me. I want Father to live.

When the second and final Du'a is over, and I have lifted my palms in gratitude, head bowed in submission, and shaken hands with the person to my right, then my left, I stand in queue for holy water poured in tiny, sparkling white cups shaped like tulips. Grandmother takes her time, whispering into her cup. Downstairs, I have Grandmother's sandals ready. Grandfather and my brother are waiting in our combat-coloured Peugeot. Both have dined at the Dodoma Hotel. Perfect Jane Austen time, Grandmother comes down thirty minutes later, and I set her sandals by her feet. Grandfather says she cannot bear to leave without socializing. Grandmother says politeness is essential to keep things breezy. I keep out.

When darkness plunges, the mill barely runs now. Instead, in the evenings, my brother terrorizes me, hiding behind the mango and jamun trees when ghosts are on their promenade. When we ask for presents, Grandfather slaps his knee as if the deed is already done. He is fidgety. But on Wednesday nights, 9 p.m., after the jamatkhana, Grandfather, Grandmother, Brother, and I all go to Ramson's Cinema to see cowboy films.

In the hush of red, velvet drapery, Father disappears.

The women of Dodoma have a soft corner for cowboys who are crybabies at a mother's feet, but who are also extirpators of injustice and perspicacious as wise kings. Grandmother and I are connoisseurs of cowboy heroes; we like Giuliano Gemma from *One Silver Dollar*. He has curly hair and his teeth are not long and aloof like Mr. Clint Eastwood's. Indian heroes and Giuliano Gemma are crybabies. We like them that way. Flint-eyed Clint leaves us cold. He truly does ride off into the sunset, his needle jaw set. Grandmother and I like a cowboy who rides off steely-backed, but then does a roundabout for the girl. With the pomegranate sun slanting on his face, Giuliano Gemma rides off into the sunset, but with a ripple moving under his strong cheek. An Indian hero, meanwhile, has podgy jowls, like the actor Feroz Khan, palmed and balmed by his personal barber, aunty-fans wanting to pinch his fleshy cheeks.

Maa says, "Such softness ought to be smothered with pistachios—like a creamy Indian sweet, with edible silver, nutty in the middle, and pale as gloves on the outside. A decadent delight!"

Giuliano Gemma swallows, does cowboy talk with his cheek. Cat whistles soar from the frontbenchers. Rose attar wafts from behind Grandmother's hot ears.

Giuliano Gemma is turning back. The brief moment stretches in slow motion, horse and rider riding wavelike toward the settlement. Frontbenchers in Ramson's Cinema bob up and down, knocking their bums on the cheap seats.

The screen glows.

"Come on brother, go to her," the frontbenchers coax Giuliano Gemma. Hands cupped around their mouths, they croon, "Malaika, nakupenda, Malaika." Nakupenda in straitlaced Swahili means, "I love you," but underneath, it is wilder than love. "Angel, I love you, my Angel."

Up on the balcony and in the boxes, we root as well, Dodoma Ascot style. Women press white handkerchiefs to their mouths and maintain dignified immobility. Our rare, prickly bird continues to be serenaded. And for a while, upstairs and downstairs are bonded well-wishers.

Our hero stops at the edge of the settlement. By the fence post, a slender girl is waiting for him. She knows he will return. Throughout the film, she only spoke to him with her purple jamun eyes, harder than kisses.

Most days of the week, Dodoma only needs one hairdresser. But on Fridays and Sundays, three would be saluted. On Fridays, the hairdresser is the busiest with women from our community. They come to the jamatkhana dressed to the nines. Many like to leave their heads uncovered, unlike women at the Sikh gurdwara or the Hindu temple. Then, on Sunday mornings, it is the turn of other women to visit the hairdresser. The hairdresser is a spinster who did her hairstylist's course in Nairobi. She wears a pink coat. When she pumps her swivelling black chair up and down, her mouth, already vague as Eid's sliver of a moon, disappears entirely. Women like their hair done in petals. The hairdresser backcombs a strip of hair and sprays it with VO5 hairspray. Then, with a flick of her long-tailed comb, twirls the hair into a plump petal. Sometimes jasmines and roses are woven in. Grandmother's dislike for baby's breath is made known: "With a name like baby's breath, you know there is something creepy round the corner."

Sunday is the day that all women dress up for the cinema. Mrs. Bhajaj, Jena Bai, Grandmother, and other women shimmer in their very best. (Tall Woman has never been seen at Ramson's Cinema.)

One Sunday, when Saira Banu onscreen is lazing by a fountain of pink water, wearing jewels thick as a rolled rug, and servers in melon-coloured turbans bring her platters of fruit, Grandfather asks Grandmother, "Is this the fifth or sixth song?"

"Third, my love."

A hit Hindi film has ten to twelve song-and-dance numbers.

Grandfather feels the story in such films, one rife with coincidences, sprouts in all directions like armpit hair. But what irritates Grandfather soothes me.

The heroine constantly sacrifices. Like what happened before Intermission in today's film was the heroine clutched the villain's leather-jacketed arm and told the hero to leave her alone, that she never loved him. She loved the villain. The suffering hero headed to a seedy bar. He sang a long, sad song and downed an entire bottle of Johnny Walker. When he returned home, his sick mother gave him a hurler of a slap. Good boys did not smoke nor drink. The hero wept. Paradise was at a mother's feet.

Now, finally, the truth is out: the heroine broke up with the hero to secretly save him from the villain. The hero and heroine are in each other's arms again. When the hero looks up at the sky, blue gods with pursty red lips smile down, their palms raised in blessing.

My brother swings his legs in anticipation, waiting for Grand-father to whisk him off from torture. And after the third dance, Grandfather's restlessness is palpable. Grandmother draws his face close and whispers in his ear. Their faces close together are like a bride and groom's in the photographs in Robert's Studio. Grand-father lets out a low laugh.

If Mother were here, I would say to her, why can we not return to Tukuyu, have a happy ending? Like the comet we saw in Tukuyu, Father is becoming a novelty. Did my brother and I really see it? Father was not sick then. We had supper on patio chairs. Father said we had to watch carefully because the comet would not appear again for years. When I finally saw it, I was disappointed. It had a long tail of a tadpole with a fuzzy, silvery light. In comparison, cows returning home from the forest at night were more like creatures from outer space. In the darkness, their eyes glittered blue. The only familiar thing about the spooky herd was the tinkling bells around their necks.

I want to hold my brother's hand, but he would shriek. His mop of brown hair, the way he carefully parks his bicycle behind Grand-father's desk in the Dead Office, already I miss him, though he is right beside me.

Grandfather is up, grabbing my brother's hand.

"I've had it!" he exclaims.

Kartar Singh, the Sikh carpenter, rises up as well. Kartar Singh is another unconventional person in town, and a fan of Grandfather's. He rides his lorry everywhere, even to the movies. When he blows his nose he uses his hands, the slimy, grey passion fruit all over his fingers. Grandfather never shirks from shaking hands; so when Maa takes a good look at his hands, she insists he take a bath.

Kartar Singh gave Jimmy-Jinxed a job when he was discharged from Dodoma Mental. Jimmy-Jinxed was at Dodoma Mental forever, even during the time of the British. But then Dr. Glyster arrived from Manchester, which, to us, was London. Dr. Glyster tried to correct us on many occasions, but Dublin, Glasgow, or Manchester could also be referred to as "London." The Queen's was the most powerful currency in the world, and because it rained in London everyday, Tanzanians who returned home, had pale green skins, and spoke tip-top English like the Queen herself acquired the coveted title of "London Returned." Sometimes Dr. Glyster, tall as a giraffe and friendly with everyone, lost his patience. Sharpness crept into his tone. *Manchester was not London.* But that did not make a lick of difference to us. Dr. Glyster, whose hair comes down his shoulders. Our hairdresser calls it "that hair." She says she would love to grab and lop off "that hair."

Dr. Glyster treats patients like they are his pals. So one day, Jimmy-Jinxed told the doctor, "I need to find a job," and Dr. Glyster permitted him to leave. Jimmy-Jinxed still wears the hospital's white drawstring pants and cotton top, even at work. Mr. Kartar Singh says he can wear a blue dress for all he cares as long as he does his job well. Everyone in town knows Jimmy-Jinxed's furniture, simple with long lines, like prayer cleanliness.

"Kazi yako!" Kartar Singh cheers when Grandfather rises up. In Swahili, the phrase means, "You showed them," a kind of applause for a mate who has demonstrated grit. Indian males in Tanzania like to use this phrase when pumped up.

"Count me in as well, brothers! I cannot stop scratching my ass out of boredom!" That is Mr. Fathlo, the town's comedian.

Women titter, as if to say, what do you expect from a man who has two wives? The two wives seated beside Mr. Fathlo call each other "sister." Mr. Fathlo's nickname is Johnny Walker. Although, he does not look anything like Johnny Walker, the Hindi screen comedian.

While Mr. Fathlo has a minty face and long, floppy buttocks, Johnny Walker's face has betel nut hardness and he sports a Robert Mugabe moustache. His dimpled chin is a perch, twitched upward like a Barbara Cartland heroine. But in a small town, anyone who wears a poncho right off is Clint Eastwood from *The Good, the Bad and the Ugly*. And so, in Dodoma, Mr. Fathlo with his two wives, because he is automatically the butt of jokes, is nicknamed Johnny Walker.

The crowd of men head downstairs for a treat of broiled, bite-sized beef served with tamarind chutney. The hawkers outside Ramson's Cinema do a brisk business, even when the film is playing. With no time to look up, they smirk into the food they serve. I hear the conversations from my brother, who mimics the men faultlessly.

"Does the sisterfucker of a director think we are fools?"

"You tell me. Only in a Hindi film a policeman wears a vampire's cloak. Do you see a policeman wrapped in such comical attire in an English film? English films are true reality."

"I see English films only for the French kiss."

"Careful, you motherfucker, can't you see we have kids about?"

With the men out of the way, there is instant relief among the women. Grandmother's duty of keeping Grandfather in his seat is over. Along with the rest of the women, she abandons herself to the film. It is as if the women have locked the bathroom door from the inside to take a leisurely bath with scented soap they stashed away for moments like this, to be left alone.

Tomorrow, Monday, will be the busiest day of the week for the Sonara. He gets a steady trail of women at his shop, inspired by jewellery worn by the heroines in the films. For the women, Indian films are Dodoma's *Elle*. In addition to being tickled by the song-and-dance fare, the women are immersed in an intense workshop, jotting design to memory, or stamping a blouse colour into their eye. At the next wedding, a woman will make a grand entrance in a sari the shade of a moonstone tinged with hues of glassy rose. Breathlessly she will let on that she was inspired by the colour scheme of a heroine's sari. That is all she will reveal, no more. When pressed, the woman will continue her breathless laugh, but carry the secret to her grave. When the same pendant or bracelet design is sought by more than three women, it tacitly falls upon the Sonara to steer the next woman towards another creation. He coaxed Jena Bai, Grandfather's 'sister', to forget about a bangle design she wanted. Instead, he made her a heavy hairpin with a tiny locket that carried a secret message from her husband-to-be.

During siesta, if the Sonara is not with Grandmother then most likely he is at Ramson's Cinema, a fan whirring above his head, intent on the heroine's armlet or choker of which his customers will demand replicas.

After three hours of cathartic crying at Ramson's Cinema, the women sighing, "Indeed God is great," Sunday nights we return home. Grandmother puts food away, mixes Ovaltine in hot milk for all of us. Grandfather does not want to spoil Grandmother's soft mood and this is the only time he drinks milk. Their movements are tender. Then he locks the doors. I put my books in the satchel ready for Monday and set my brother's uniform on a chair. In bed, I pat Brother's stomach, occasionally blow on it to remove any evil eye. In the mornings, it takes him ages to put on his socks. He stares at the wall, sock in hand. So sometimes at bedtime I pull his socks up his legs, ready for morning, his docile eyes watching me. I resume patting his stomach until he is sleepy.

Brother and I both go to the Aga Khan Primary School where everyone is a fan of Muhammad Ali. But Brother is more interested in the one who races, rather than floats, his car buzzing through three feet of water. Bert Shankland, winner of the 1966 East African Safari Rally, the toughest course over roads in Kenya, Uganda, and Tanzania. In the past, mostly Kenyan drivers won the grand silver trophy. They would sit on the hoods of their cars, swigging champagne out of bottles. My brother's admiration for Shankland rises after the floods of 1966 put Shankland to the test with river swellings, mudslides, and route changes. His car swam and raced and flew.

Waiting for Grandfather or Grandmother to tuck us in, switch off the lights, Brother quizzes me.

"Where does the Rally begin?"

"Nairobi."

"Who flags off the rally?"

"Mzee Jomo Kenyatta, the President of Kenya."

"Who is Shankland's co-driver?"

I shrug.

"Chris Rothwell. They raced in a Volvo PV 544?"

There are enough numbers and letters about the car. I say, "Yes."

"Wrong! I'll give you a clue. It's what Grandfather drives."

"A Peugeot.

"Yes, they raced in a Peugeot 404. Grandfather's is a 403 model. Where did Bert Shankland collect most of his points in the rally?"

"Easy-peasy. In the muddy Usambara Mountains of Tanzania."

Grandfather wants to take my brother to Arusha for the next East African Safari Rally. "You can meet Shankland and Rothwell," Grandfather says tucking us in.

I tell Brother I will be right here, at Grandparents', waiting for him to return.

I close my eyes and send Father and Mother on a holiday, far away to Shanghai, San Francisco, or Muscat. I return to Ramson's Cinema.

I pair Giuliano Gemma with Saira Banu who went to a finishing school in Switzerland. She will understand the touchy cowboy. Behind my closed eyelids, the screen goddess glides by a lush grove wearing hoarfrost anklets and a moonstone-studded cummerbund. Under the canopy of soothing green opulence, her movements are atoning as the bulbous sway of an elephant.

Ramson's Cinema makes grief bearable.

When Saira Banu's glass bangles break into crescents against the rebel-hero's chest, clouds in the sky clang, a peacock dances razzmatazz on a rooftop, and Saira sings, "If I slip-and-slide today, don't lift me up." Woozily, I remember that when the hero caressed Saira Banu's plump thigh in the rain, Grandfather nudged Grandmother, like, should I be watching this? Grandmother snorted, patted his hand, impatient to return to the film.

I am never casual about shortening its name. I whisper, "Goodnight, Ramson's Cinema," full name respect.

Before Allah Troubles You,
First He Will Seek Your Permission

Kenya is another country. To get to Nairobi, you have to cross the border after Arusha-with-red-soil, home of the Masai. Like heroes who win their brides in archery contests, a young Masai is only permitted to marry after he kills a lion.

Buses refuse to have the Masai aboard. They reek of cow dung that they mix with soil and smear on their bodies and braided hair. Their only pieces of clothing are ochre cloths tied in knots around their shoulders and catwalk leather belts about their waists for money pouches; they carry sheathed knives. The Masai are slender giants over six feet tall. Since childhood, beaded chokers are pushed down their necks, one after another, to lengthen them regal.

In our house, there is reverence and wariness for the reddish-brown Masai. Nairobi, so close, is a place where Father may get better or die. The name "Nairobi" comes from the Masai for cool waters.

"There's nothing cooling in their deeds or words," Mzee Mamudu says. No admiration from him.

He is teaching me to roll out chapattis. "You are as bad as your father," he tells me. "Both of you turn out imperfect circles."

When I smile, he says, "You have your grandmother's chalky smile, but she is no shirker. Mama has always given that Masai stinker her due. She told your uncle, 'I am Big-Mother. She is Small-Mother.' One does not need Ganga magic to know which mother your uncle prefers."

In Swahili lore, a Small-Mother is not like Uncle's. She is soft as meat coming off the bone. She is usually young, often poor, from the village, and marries a much older, affluent man-of-the-house and joins his family in town. The Big-Mother may be already old or sick. Small-Mother is the rescuer who mutes her own grievances and takes over household chores in her new home. With the children, she is an indulgent grown-up sister. Most senior women of the family do not say a word when Small-Mother plays hopscotch with other children, or when she cannot control her laughter. These are her days to play and enjoy, they say. Only when the man-of-the-house favours her outright does a Big-Mother lose her milky kindness for a Small-Mother.

"The husband's indiscretions are his own fault, curdling milk in an already good household. Then there are sons who curdle their own mother's milk. Your uncle thinks that stinker covered in red dung is better than the mama who gave him birth! Your uncle arrived home already under her spell. What did your grandmother do? She quietly roped her milkless breasts with her own intestines and declared the stinker her son's Small-Mother."

Why is Mzee Mamudu saying "*your* uncle," "*your* uncle," like it is my fault?

Orange, the hue of home, is not always sunny. What else happened to Uncle there, in Masai country, no one asks him for fear he may completely slip away from us.

Whenever Uncle leaves Dodoma for Masai country, Grandfather requests that Mzee Mamudu get tea snacks from the Maharajah Hotel. He rings up the Sonara and tells him, "Your sister," he means Grandmother, "needs some cheering."

"What about Grandfather?" I ask Mzee Mamudu.

"Oh, he gave up on your uncle when he broke his mama's heart."

"He does not like Uncle or Father," I say. Mzee Mamudu keeps quiet. "Father expects Mother, me, and my brother to be strong. Did Grandfather hold Grandmother in his arms when Uncle told them about his Masai mother? Did he?"

"No, each must bear his own pain; otherwise, no one can get up the next day."

Home cannot imbibe all the grief and not explode. Bits of

anguish and suffering, like shards, like bubbles on roasted flesh, must be borne alone, even in a household of potato ducks with saffron worms dangling from their beaks, of noodles lovingly cooked and strewn with almonds lavish as though delivered by a Mogul emperor's hand. Some rope their breasts with their own intestines. Others hide grief at the nape. Silent transactions continue. Dwellers converge at the kitchen table or in the veranda. Mzee Mamudu sweeps up dead mice, their pelts still shiny, along with lizard dung and thick grey dust. Twice a day, mornings and evenings, he swishes poison in steamy water and mops the floors with the sternness of de-lousing. Only mangoes ripen golden in the torpor of Dodoma's heat. Life goes on.

For months, the mill is almost silent. In secret, Grandmother hands over her gold to the Sonara so that my brother and I can fly to Nairobi to see Father. Gold she purchased from the Sonara on her fenced-off afternoons, before President Nyerere adopted Chairman Mao's model of back to the farms, before property became a feudal word, before Indians began leaving Tanzania, before the arrival of Maxwell Bath Soap, one kind of soap from the People's Republic of China.

"Be vigilant, Sister. Your dark times have woken from slumber," the Sonara warns Grandmother. Grandmother hands over her private fortune to her trusted friend, hush, not a word breathed to Grandfather. First time, she locks her bedroom door. I am the sentry posted outside.

The Sonara's ancestral home is in Surat, in Gujarat. He receives blue airmail letters monthly. After nationalization of properties, Mwalimu Nyerere's African youth are ecstatic, shouting up and down Main Street that in ninety-nine percent African Tanzania, one percent Indian, the bloodsuckers cannot own all the property. For me the word "ancestral" is paradisiacal, an airy dwelling with sky blue windows. Nothing snatched away, but razzmatazz kingfishers quivering on tall trees. Lanterns lit at the end of the day. Not like Dodoma of dusty, ragged birds, kitchen drawers to be cleaned every two days because of cockroaches.

The town waits for our mill to become government property. That will shut off the Lion, they say. Grandfather walks about in town, collars dashed up. He has already proved up. So what if the government contracts have stopped?

Death hovers above Father's head.

There is a mad reek of jasmines coming from Grandmother's bedroom.

I hear Grandmother and the Sonara talking.

"I even blow on buttermilk now that I have been scalded. We do not know what will happen to my son-in-law. The town watching our every move and now Nyerere nationalizing property like toys, everyone striking when the iron is hot."

"So did Kaikeyi," the Sonara says, drawing from the *Ramayana*.

It's the same old story. Kaikeyi, the arch stepmother, demanded of her husband that her own son, *not* Rama the golden, become the next successor. The ailing king had once promised Kaikeyi, young and dimple-cheeked, a boon that she held in the hem of her silken garments for years until Rama was about to become king, and then she demanded her boon.

Grandmother concurs, "Indeed, so did Kaikeyi."

Examples from Hindu scriptures lend Grandmother solace. Our forefathers were Hindus, our hymns and rituals are more Hindu than Arab-Islam.

When the pain in her back isn't burning, she jokes with the Sonara, saying the knots are light as the Carrick bend ones he designs for his Christian customers. At his shop, the Sonara has a glass compartment, narrow as a flutist's lips, for bracelets and chains with slim knots for Goans and the British. They prefer wispy jewellery to ornate designs in twenty-four karat gold.

Fasting for Grandfather's well being, for Father's life, singing hymns with the congregation where allegory is richly Hindu, lighting incense, drinking holy water from a tulip cup dissolves the knots in Grandmother's back. It centres her. It is total submission to Allah, the dorky, unhinged devotion of Grandfather's, that Grandmother cannot manage. She chokes when he sings:

Before Allah troubles you
First
He will seek your permission.

The door unlocks and the Sonara slips on his waistless shoes. His feet are oblong scrubbing brushes. Although he walks everywhere, his heels are pale as a priest's. I stare at his feet. I always do. The veins on his arch doing an eel frolic, boinking up and down. I tell Maa his designs come from his feet, as I have told her many times. Each time she listens as if they are a sage's words. She knows instinct with jewels is sacred, not to be scoffed at. I sense, as I would a ghost behind me, that if I touch his instep, my fingers will shoot up fires. The jamun droops; the lotus pendants sultry as hips; the thorns studded with sapphires; Dodoma's bitter moon on a smirched ruby, they come from the fecund patches on his feet. When he walks, his feet barely touch the ground.

His shoes on, the Sonara pats my head and tells Grandmother, "Do not fret, Sister. Do you not see the goddess of fortune is guarding your door?" He means me.

"Your possessions are in my keep only temporarily," he tells her, raising the bundle of gold, three precious knots on the top. Lakshmi of fortune will get them back to you, but when and where, Sister, is in the goddess's hands."

The Sonara leaves. I ask Grandmother, "Is my father going to die?"

Grandmother draws me very close. "Speak gor gor sweet, my child. Be smooth as a sliding door. Allah is kind and merciful. Still, why draw His attention our way?"

I will be like Grandmother. I will be a sliding door.

Just as with a young girl who will grow up to be dancer, whose trainer pinches and flexes her limbs and her narrow back to make her supple, Grandmother trains me when to slip and slide and change, and when to remain inert. She tells me, "It is true, women are the keepers. We are keepers of silverware, the bite of savouries in our broth. We are the sole keepers of the keys to the almari. But child, what we really excel at is adapting. Outward, we appear fixed, planted as feet, but we are also amphibians, pulling our families through land and sea when catastrophe strikes."

In the *Mahabharata*, the king, Prince Bhisma's father, is in love with a fisherman's beautiful daughter. The fisherman's condition is that the king may only marry his daughter if their future son, and not Bhisma, the king's first born and true successor, be the next king.

Bhisma takes a vow of celibacy. His sacrifice of putting his father's desires before his own even pleases the gods. To Amba, however, the explanation is codswallop. Resolute in her decision, she jumps into a fire she wills and dies. In each of her reincarnations, her single purpose is to be Bhisma's killer. At nights, she enters his dreams, "Bhisma, Bhisma, Bhisma," she rattles his name with dry, open eyes.

Grandmother's whisper: "Best to withdraw when Allah has decided."

We are rushed to Robert's Studio for passport photographs. Grandmother pulls chunky sweaters over our heads, "To steel you from the cold even before you get there," she tells us. "Nairobi is cold as London." But I know she wants my brother and me to each look as chubby as the baby on the tin for Farex biscuits. Even though we are not babies anymore. She adores Father, her son-in-law. Night after night, she prays wheezy prayers to save him. In the morning, her mouth stinks.

In her wedding photographs, Mother stands by Father, already his shoulder-boulder, not like a bride with wispy collarbones. There are no photographs of Grandmother when she got married, but it is easy to imagine her, a trim-waisted, fluttery bride. On her visits to Tukuyu, Grandmother would twirl the long stretch of Father's arm and fold up on his chest like a closed-winged butterfly.

Grandmother's gold pays for Father's hospitalization and our plane ride to the big cancer hospital in Nairobi, where my brother and I receive lunch bag treats of red apples and green grapes, costly fruit that even Grandfather purchases with solemnity at Household and Sundries. On hospital benches, we swing our feet in new Bata shoes and munch on exotic fruit. Each apple is wrapped in crinkly tinsel that I save in my Enid Blyton books, opening apple-scented mystery pages.

Tart fruit and cancer smell.

My brother and I are in Father's face, pinning him down.

Grandmother told us that we are the sharpest weapons. A man will do anything to live for his children, weakening Yama of Death. Punching hard, dry kisses on our cheeks, Grandmother said, "Goodbye, my heroes," before we climbed the rickety staircase of the Dakota airplane to pull Father back.

The long, threadlike stranger lying in bed has green cheeks. My brother looks at me.

Mother takes us to the hospital garden to see the fishpond and waterfalls. There are no milkmen in Nairobi delivering milk on bicycles, two steel milk cans hanging on their handlebars. We drink milk from triangle milk cartons with green swirls of lollipop design. The nurse brings us straws.

We are quiet children. When Father is asleep, my brother and I lie in our cots. Mother is studying her palms, her somnambulist face gone away.

Yama of Death doesn't arrive that night. Next morning, Father wakes up. His eyes following us. There is a moist odour in the room, meatish, ripening, but also rotted. We spend our time in the hospital garden. In less than five days we return to Dodoma.

The mighty retch of the mill does not start at 5:30 in the mornings any more. The long pipes connected to grinders and chutes are flaccid like trunks on dead elephants. During the day, one machine is switched on. Government contracts have stopped. When a few orders straggle in from upcountry, our lorries topple like toys on roads smooth and dry as the Sahara.

"When Allah yields our way again, He will tear down our rooftop with abundance," Grandfather promises Grandmother.

"And I, a good Muslim, must submit and watch," Grandmother retaliates.

Coming out of the bathroom after watering his roses, Grandfather's whispers to Allah are tutti-frutti, sometimes a thrum, and always mixed with his saliva, this part of the holy Du'a:

> I prostrate before Thee
> I rely upon Thee
> From Thee is my strength
> And Thou art my protection.

Grandmother's prayers are organized. Like a good algebra student, she starts at the beginning:

> In the name of Allah, the most beneficent, the most merciful.

My brother and I are treated like royalty. Grandfather takes us for rides outside Dodoma at 1 a.m. The moon is wildly orange. When we hear the sinister cooing of the hyenas, we clutch each other out of the pleasure of fear. In six hours, I have to get ready for school. I am floating, not bound to rules. Grandmother does not blink when I tell her that at a birthday party I filched cake for my brother, or when I tell her that a while ago, I took a shilling from her purse to put under Brother's pillow when he lost his tooth. In the bathroom, he wiggles his naked bum close to the steaming urn, grinning, daring me to grab him. When I do, I hit him hard. When I see a boy with toffee brown hair crossing Main Street on his own, I tear after him. But my brother is in the veranda riding his red bicycle.

One time, just after I had returned from school, he was upright on his saddle, hands crossed and tucked under his armpits. "Look, no hands!" he said. I burst into tears. Mzee Mamudu was displeased, "The boy has been waiting all day to show you his mastery, and you cry! What kind of a sister are you!"

What if my brother collided into a lamppost? Another thing to dread.

At the post office, when we place a call to Nairobi, Mother comes over the crackling lines, startled.

"Are you fine, Mother?" I ask.

Tukuyu's butter sunlight pouring through the living room window after a fog, Mother's knitting needles, and the open-faced

Life magazines on the sofa are like parts of a fading dream, are like ways-a-way in China. I remember snippets, like once when I peeped through the toilet keyhole, Father was sitting on a big crate with a doughnut hole in the middle, reading. The real toilet was underneath. How old was my brother then? He was young enough to like wearing my sundresses. I also got white patches on my cheeks. Mother gave me medicine. Next morning, a big, dead worm came out when I went to the toilet.

After we return from Nairobi, as more and more Indians start leaving Tanzania, Grandfather continues to sing Sufi lyrics with cavernous passion. Merrily he submits to Allah, in the bathroom, or while nursing his double-peg of Chivas. Allah is a luminous beauty with a mane of frothy curls. Grandfather is the impassioned lover.

The bathroom door swings open. Grandfather does not stop singing:

> Let me live, lovely one.
>
> Do not tease me, for my chest is already bloody.

"What can I say, child?" Grandmother says. "Being frolicsome with Allah is your Grandfather's way."

> I prostrate before Thee.
>
> I rely upon Thee.

Grandfather prays continuously.

Grandfather is Tanzania's unclaimed patriot. His rivals want to take him down a peg or two. They do not care for his hob-knobbing with Hindus, Sikhs, Sunnis, the Goans, the local Gogos of Dodoma, the Warangis from near Kondoa, and the few Chaggas like Uncle Chando. Grandfather's rivals, particularly the Indian Shopkeeper-with-Red-Lips, detest Grandfather making a messy omelette, mixing everyone together. Never spoken aloud to his face, messages are brought to Grandmother by Mama Titi or Jena Bai, our grandparents' friends: that Grandfather has a thick coconut for a skull, too dumb to grasp that Indians do not scramblify, let alone melt in other pots. When Grandfather's allies meet in the Dead Office to tell him this, Mzee Mamudu wipes the furniture with a wet cloth and shoos the dogs off into the veranda. They report what is openly drumming in town. That is: surround the mighty Lion and stick his hoity tail up his hoity ass. Grandfather wants to visit the Indian Shopkeeper-with-Red-Lips.

"No, not to confront but to convince him," he tells his allies.

His allies warn him it would be a foolish mistake. Who can stop Grandfather?

He asks his allies, "Why would anyone want to continue living blindly like a one-eyed mullah when Tanzania is all shook up for change?"

Grandmother warns him plenty as well, "I know of your sincerity, but it comes out gaudy as a fête. Speak gor gor sweet, my love." Grandfather swings her in his arms, whether serenading Maa or Allah with the glorious curls, I can't tell:

> Your pout
> Your pale gestures
> I beseech you
> Stab your gaze elsewhere.

"You've gone crazy as a coot," Grandmother tells him.

"I wonder if the Indian Shopkeeper-with-Red-Lips complained of whisky on my breath?" he asks her.

"My love, I am sure he did. How could he digest his Friday prayers otherwise?"

"Whose business is it if I kneel on whisky-dimpled knees for my beloved Allah?"

Grandfather has started taking the marimba to the bathroom, plucking music on the metal wires on top of the wooden box like a goat herder. Often Grandmother puts her ear to the door. If he is singing of Allah's creamy torso, she knows he is all right. Grandmother is not feather-light watching over her husband. She is the Lioness.

The mill has shrivelled and the growl of lorries has gone. One day, Grandfather has the majestic door opened, joining one of the teams of pullers, strutting his frame like a footballer. Does he want the door opened to lift our gloom? Grandmother careens her neck anxiously. Almost half of Dodoma can look right into our veranda when the door of our granary is pulled open. Is it Grandfather's intention to dispatch to town his cocky message of "Just watch me?"

"During such times, it is prudent to sip even cool buttermilk with caution," Grandmother reminds him. She might as well be talking to the wind.

One morning, right after breakfast, when Grandmother is braiding my hair for school, Mama Titi and Jena Bai come over to report that Grandfather has told off a bunch of monied Indian shopkeepers not willing to boost black Tanzanians' credit privileges.

"What did he say?" she asks.

"That independence, a free Tanzania, has only emerged on the doorstep of his mill," Mama Titi informs her.

"Mama, the Lion said, 'White Sahibs did not want Brown Sahibs, now Brown Sahibs do not want Black Sahibs,'" adds Jena Bai.

They answer her other question as well, that yes, Shopkeeper-with-Red-Lips was there as well, but said nothing.

"What was the shy dik-dik waiting for?" Maa asks sarcastically.

"Waiting for us to pass the message to the mistress of the house, Sister," Jena Bai tells her.

In front of the town of Dodoma, Grandmother is a daughter-in-law, bobbing her head to one and all. At home, her fasts for Grandfather's welfare increase. She blows fragrant, green prayers on his forehead and counsels him steadily.

"My love, do not be a child who insists today is Eid, who wants his presents now."

"So now I'm a child? You are being unjust! So busy are we making money and looking out at the Indian Ocean to India of our ancestors that we have not learned the names of birds and plants here, and we have been here for three hundred years, quite a while, will you not agree? I'm no child. I'm proving up. Why are the Ribeiros of today hiding?"

Grandfather's hero, Dr. Rosendo A. Ribeiro, is the Goan-Nairobian who returned to Nairobi at the turn of the twentieth century after his medical training in Great Britain and did his rounds on the back of a docile zebra.

Grandfather is like Tall Woman in his doggedness. Both single-minded as Amba. Amba cannot be persuaded by Prince Bhisma's reasoning. He cannot marry her because of his vow of celibacy. Grandfather does not heed the counsel of his well-wishers. And he is not wily. If he were, perhaps he could have persuaded some of the town-wallahs over to his side, strengthening their dreams instead of rattling their anxieties ever more in Nyerere's revolution of shared property. Mwalimu, in love with Chairman Mao, thinks an Africa of olden times is possible, when wealth was shared equally amongst everyone. Now Grandfather is beginning to say that Mwalimu has gone soft in the head to want to celebrate the Chinese New Year in Tanzania.

Grandfather's uncomplicated finger is not on the pulse of the wind's gait, which way her health is blowing, blossoming.

Then the moment finally comes.

Grandfather and I are in the shop of Shopkeeper-with-Red-Lips. He sells ribbons, wedding lace, watches, shoe polish, and hair dyes.

"Good afternoon, Bwana Lion," Shopkeeper-with-Red-Lips greets him.

Grandmother has deftly avoided Shopkeeper at the jamatkhana and on the streets. Not Grandfather. Whatever he has to say, he will say up front. If Grandfather, the beatnik, is one end of the town of Dodoma, Shopkeeper-with-Red-Lips is the other end. He won't even drink a glass of water from other Indians not from our community.

Today is Shopkeeper's day.

"Bwana Lion, the fortune you must have made from government contracts that your grandchildren are flying in smart Dakotas to Nairobi to see their father, while we are still paying with cowries like junglees in the forest. By the way, Sir, how is your son-in-law?"

Shopkeeper has cast the first stone. The sinner, Grandfather, is a tattered Lion. Everyone knows the mill is at a standstill. Even I understand tattered lions have no business roaring or being shamelessly bulky.

Grandfather does not grab Shopkeeper by the collar. Give Grandfather a dead, rubbery goat's head to play polo with, Uzbekistan style, and he will play with a mean, snatching force. But he does not know how to play to get even. He is no match for cruel Shopkeeper who is dancing on our calamity.

"The child's father is dying," Grandfather tells Shopkeeper, his bulky paw rubbing my ear.

I pull at Grandfather's hand and we vacate Shopkeeper's premises. I do not let go of his hand, very sure of the path home.

At the jamatkhana.

Smack.

A man peoned by a rival miller beseeches Grandfather, sitting in the front, to move to the back.

"Perhaps the Lion will be more comfortable by the ample walls for support. A thousand apologies for the inconvenience, but the Lion is barricading the view of meagre men from Allah."

Grandfather heaves himself up from floor. He leaves the jamatkhana, forever.

Grandmother consoles him, "Allah is great. My love, be thankful your feet had not gone to sleep."

"Then I would have inevitably fallen flat on my remarkable spread," replies Grandfather.

"And they would have mixed sugar with dal and rice and distributed it as if Bibi Fatima, the Prophet's very daughter, had come to them in their dreams," Grandmother says.

"But my love, it was not their lucky day."

The bathroom door continues to swing open. Grandfather, pink as rose, singing away:

Tease me no more,

I am done in.

Does he mean he is done in by the town of Dodoma?

Or by the mill?

Is he done in by Allah who rides on his breath?

Or by Mother, soon to be widowed? Nothing is harder on a man than to witness his daughter having a widow's smell.

That Mama Has Big Buttocks

I was three when the British left in 1961. Then, from Tanganyika to Tanzania: I have known the country as Tanzania. The sound of its name, crisp, like its sleeves are rolled up, ready for business. The island of Zanzibar joined the country. Part of its name included in the new Tanzania. Tanganyika of the Germans and the British is mellow, a story of the past in an old, yellowing photograph.

I like Koti Kamanga, Uncle Chando's nephew from Moshi, who is new to our school. His mother is from Congo where they speak French, so Koti is already exotic. We are in the same class. He wears purple socks to school and spells dictionary words with an unsquashy calm. But even I know that Africa is for the Africans. Our mill has still not been nationalized. Grandfather being cocksure no one can touch him. He has proved up. I cannot fight Mzee Mamudu and take it out on Koti because he likes me back, boy-girl. The day after Mzee Mamudu planted his feet firmly in his kitchen, defying Grandmother, letting Motor Mouth on the radio go on panting like a roly-poly Indian woman making dirty noises, I told Koti that black politicians are a pack of hyenas, no, worse, they are black pigs. We do not let our knees touch under the long desk we share.

Indians do not speak Swahili syrupy like the islanders of Zanzibar. Theirs is juice flowing from behind the molars. But in the interior of the country, it is different. For many, Swahili is the language of fetch and carry, of never putting honest change in a housewife's palm after purchases. Most Indian mummies and daddies want their children to speak tally-ho English, but, after nationalization, Indians make an effort to become African.

Grandfather says, "Sure, bring on the water to douse the fire that has already spread." To him, proving up has come too late. "From our small shops, we never bothered to look up until Nyerere's Revolution hit us in the face." Now Indian women attend parties in native kitenge dresses but cannot jiggle their hips and breasts with abandon, like Mama Titi, K. K. Alps. They dance like Indian women, with pinched restrain, another screaming tickler for black Tanzanians.

Before independence, we were the middlemen between the British and the Africans, starting small, opening shops in the boonies. When we looked up, it was in the direction of a town to settle in, like Tukuyu, then the bigger towns of Mbeya, Arusha, and Dodoma. When the British left, Indians took over, the new masters in charge of businesses, transportation, newspapers, buildings—nowadays, harangued by Mwalimu's youths.

Indians do not scramblify easily, but stick to mother country like chewing gum under a desk. For pish-posh education, we go to Great Britain and become barristers and doctors. Marriageable girls climb up the ladder two ways: go to England and return home with the title of "London Returned" and a fabulous green skin that did not see much sun in Bath or Edinburgh (London to us); or, poor but fair-skinned girls with blue-veined temples get a chance to marry into the families of business princes. The "London Returned" play tennis at the gymkhana, drink orange squash, and live on top of hills.

Now, young soldiers shove aside Grandfather's bellicose efforts to solder blacks and Indians. To them, he is an old man, a fat Indian with an incredible quartet of buttocks, no teeth in the mouth, come to hunt and roar with them.

Swahili of Small-Mother softness is spoiling for a fight. She is now the language to shake the yellow shit out of the grabby, cowardly Indians. In class, the Swahili teacher gives crude examples:

Mama yule ana matako makubwa.

That mama has big buttocks.

We know the teacher is referring to our fat Indian mothers. Koti does not snigger, but nudges his knee against mine like we are lost in the wilderness. I shrink from Small-Mother's language. When President Nyerere visits Dodoma and shakes my hand, first thing he asks me is, "Do you speak Swahili?" The way he asks, I know I am not Tanzanian. I stare at his two sawed-off incisors, his Zanaki tribal marking.

At recess, Koti and I fight a lot.

"I hate your Nyerere," I tell Koti, which is true. Koti punches my arm. My fingers tingle.

"Indians are fatty, fatty bambulas sitting on tombolas." He means Grandfather, the joke of the town. I say nothing.

Later in class, though I do not want to, I nuzzle my knee against his. He lets me.

During the afternoons, our lessons are of another kind: to run around the school compound. We shout at the top of our lungs,

> Slash the enemy!
> Slash all our enemies!

A Pakistani girl from our class is returning to Lahore. Her family does not want her to join processions in the afternoon, hoe the school's shamba, and clean the chicken coop instead of receiving lessons. I ask teacher if I could take her seat because I want a girl partner. The teacher says, "Certainly."

I begin to banish Swahili, words like "pole," which means "sorry." You say pole to a toddler who keeps falling, learning to walk. You say pole with the same lilt to a freedom fighter in jail.

No one in school tells us the story of Makhan Singh, the Punjabi-Kenyan freedom fighter, held in detention for years by the British in isolated prisons in India and Kenya. No one in school sings lullabies of the turbaned freedom fighter. It is Grandfather who tells us the story in the veranda. Uncle Chando and Grandfather sipping Chivas and us kids, including Koti, drinking Coca-Cola. We giggle about the name. Makhan is butter in Punjabi. A freedom fighter named Butter Singh.

Koti and I titter a lot. The time in Geography when the teacher asked the class "Where is Thailand?" we both pointed to our thighs and had to kneel in front of the class.

I would have been proud to see Makhan Singh's name in our primary school's orange-coloured History book. Before nationalization, we learned about Dr. Livingstone, the Rift Valley, and the slave trade, nothing about Makhan Singh or Grandfather's hero, Dr. Ribeiro, who rode to his patients' homes on a zebra.

We stand on the street and wave flags for President Tito of Yugoslavia in a white suit. He wears small, round, gold-framed dark glasses. Koti tells me he has bad teeth.

"How do you know?" I ask.

"Because after they knock back the whisky, it loosens their ties—and their ivory smiles. This is why Comrade Tito has brown teeth."

We both drink to that, carefully pushing roasted peanuts into our Coca-Cola bottles, chewing and drinking at the same time. Though we do not sit together anymore, he always waits for me after a procession.

When a mill worker touches my chest, I do not tell anyone, but I banish this time, forever.

President Nyerere makes many speeches on the radio. He says that for far too long Africa has slept, and allowed the rest of the world to walk around and over it.

There is a pair of lions at Ngorongoro National Park that Grandmother and I saw when we went to Arusha. The lioness walked around the lion, licking him, cajoling him, and Grandmother put her palm across my chest because my heart was beating. "It's beautiful, look," she whispered.

President Nyerere, his merriment spiteful, asking me, "Do you speak Swahili?" Like if I could, that would be a tickler.

Grandfather's cronies gather in the Dead Office to listen to President Nyerere's speeches. Mzee Mamudu continues to bring them trays of tea and more ice and soda for the scotch.

Grandfather tells his cronies, "Nyerere says all Indians are mnyonyajis, and 'all,' as we know, is a dangerous word."

I am hung up on the word "mnyonyaji." Lice are bloodsuckers and so are Indian shopkeepers. The phrase repeated so often. You want to puke. A hairy Indian with a tuft of hair sticking out of his ears sucking on one of Mama Titi's K. K. tits.

Grandfather says, "Screw Nyerere's policy of back to the farms. I'm a goddamn trader."

One day, a Gogo from Dodoma brings Grandfather grey powder to sprinkle underneath our giant entrance door. Grandfather had paid for his son's primary education right through his O-Levels (one of his the-right-hand-need-not-know-what-the-left-is-doing deeds). The Gogo tells Grandfather, "Mzee, a bit will do. And avoid a black man with a white dot painted on his forehead."

Suddenly, together with government contracts, people in and around Dodoma insist on having their corn and millet ground at the mill. Just as fast, Grandfather stops using the powder. That is when Grandmother comes to know the reason for our unexpected bounty. Grandfather tells her he stopped because Satan will rock your child's cradle, its devotion to its master without want, but then, even after death, there is no escaping Satan's grip. Then what? Grandfather's rage, however, is out of spite. While Indians are shaking in their shoes, Grandfather corners government officials, or gets comfortable in the middle of the sokoni. When Indians spot Grandfather among the vegetable stalls, their faces turn grim. He is hazmat, a danger to their lives. On the other hand, the Africans enjoy the distraction, grinning at the beefy old nut.

"I have a coconut for a brain because I do not get it! I mean, leave us bloodsucking Indians aside, tell me how does President Nyerere figure that Mao—that one with the meaty moon on his chin—how does he figure that his China will work in tribal Tanzania? Human beings desire palaces, not bed bunks. To share and share alike is fragrance on paper. Tell Nyerere that!"

Twice he is put in jail for inciting against the President, but in his cell, he is only deprived of his Ten Cent cigarettes. Police officers hit him with kibokos on the buttocks, but gently. The humiliation is enough, and calling him old man, asking him to hold his manners (in Swahili, good manners are held in the hem of one's garment: *hold* your manners, not *mind* your manners.)

Between jail stints, Grandfather continues to take baskets of grain to people on his private list. The Dead Office grown even more festive;

Mzee Mamudu keeps on bringing trays of chai. Grandmother tells him, "They are consuming cups of tea like Darjeeling is next door."

In the office, Grandfather pushes invoices through one of the three spikes on his table. "Let the government of donkeys figure it out," he shrugs. And, from the last jail trip, there is a sign on the wall behind his desk:

MY CATTLE ARE MINE

No punctuation, no exclamation mark at the end. That to him is an attention monger's mark. The sign is exactly what it says.

"I do not need Nyerere or his nephew Mao instructing me on mutual respect and sharing," he says.

When he was a young boy, Grandfather was given a helping hand by his uncle, already running shops in the heart of Tanzania. Now, Grandfather is doing the same, giving a helping hand to a Gogo, a Goan, or a Sikh. At a town hall meeting, he will not pipe down.

"Nephews, an Indian shopkeeper in East Africa was a pioneer, a frontier trader. The interior of Tanzania was dotted with our dukkas selling oil, soap, kerosene lanterns, spices in tiny triangle packets, matchsticks, enamel bowls and cups, salt, and mirikani cloth the Africans now use instead of animal hides to bury their dead. Ask your fathers, your grandfathers, your great-grandfathers. As soon as a lone shop opened in the middle of a jungle, activities began. Families arrived. Demands rose and businesses sprung up. Indians contributed to the development of Tanzania, but what did the British call us? 'Intensely avaricious,' but you see, my nephews, it's my Indian stupidity of not entering things in diaries like the Europeans to keep a record of what I've done for the country. Now we are called what? Bloodsuckers, that whatever I worked and struggled for, I am a bloodsucker. And in these bubbly days, my nephews, you are sprouting unripe ears, believing everything dished out, all the ting tong music from Mao."

Once again, Grandfather is hauled off to jail.

Shopkeeper-with-Red-Lips, high as a schoolgirl on a crush, says to the tea drinkers outside his shop, "Chuck the loony in the mental hospital. I will be his first visitor."

When Grandmother receives the information from her allies, she strides into his shop and slaps Shopkeeper with the back of her ringed hand.

"People and sewing machines froze. Only the dogs outside kept on fucking." That is how Jena Bai tells the story at our kitchen table years later, weaving in or unravelling a border of Dodoma's history, depending on how much gin she has poured herself in a glass. "Medicinal gin," she says, "to quell gas." She never tells the story when Grandmother is around.

Shaking his head, Grandfather tells Grandmother, "It's a mad party in there," as if she can stop the excess gaiety in the Dead Office.

One day, Uncle quietly disappears into Masai country. He never says goodbye. He asked Grandmother for the keys to her almari, helping himself to Kenyan shillings and his share of her gold, any price affordable to her as long as he remains alive. Finally, relief. It is like a relative who has at last made the choice to openly set up house with the black mistress he has been hiding in the interior for years, only Uncle set up house with his other mother.

At Dodoma Hotel, after his two pegs of whisky, Grandfather refuses to tip the waiters. "Sorry, but you must wait for the donkey government to tip you fellahs. Do not forget, when you get your tip, share it squarely amongst yourselves, including the cook, gardener, and the lavatory cleaner." Sometimes, Uncle Chando serves him to shut him up.

Grandfather continues to water his roses, feed the mild snake in the rose bin, and drive into the forest in the early hours of the morning. No matter how sleepy she is Grandmother accompanies him. My brother and I are in bed.

Both parents dead in Kutch, Gujarat, Grandfather, only a boy, was shipped off to his uncle in Tanzania to better his own prospects. The myth in Kutch being any loafer or orphan could become a mercantile prince in Africa. Just pack him off on a ship to Zanzibar, and Allah will do the rest.

Grandfather arrived when Tanzania was Tanganyika under the Germans.

His uncle had two shops in the interior.

One time, his uncle told Grandfather, then a young boy newly off the boat, to take a bale of mirikani cloth to his other shop, eight miles off. At that time, his uncle's shops were the only two shops in that part of the boonies, and the way from one shop to the other was through the forest, and always in groups with a lot of singing, hand-clapping, machetes and kibokos in hand. But Grandfather, a young boy, was sent alone.

"Not if he was the man's real son!" Grandmother says bitterly, "he would never have sent him alone!"

Whenever I hear the story, I imagine the young boy's spine tighten spiky as sisal. He knows he is being watched. From the corner of his eye, he spies a lion fifty yards off. He walks on. There is no lapsing in his gait, not even momentarily.

A boy, only nine, with a bale of mirikani across his shoulders, does not break into a run, which would make the lion change its mind. The lion has met his equal. That is what I think. Nothing to do with it being stuffed from lunch.

Grandfather and his coterie's time-pass is mocking current events, or the way they put it, "Thanks-of-a-donkey-is-a-kick." Tall Woman, whom I stood behind in the jamatkhana, has joined the cau-cus in the Dead Office, openly smoking and bringing over smuggled bottles of Chivas. She uses a cigarette holder like Rita Hayworth. As she walks past, I catch a whiff of cigarette smoke and frankincense. Mzee Mamudu likes to make her martini. Uncle Chando contrib-utes as well, filching from Dodoma Hotel's liquor supply. And most nights, at 2 a.m., with Grandmother already in the passenger seat, Grandfather drives outside Dodoma, under a canopy of thick stars. Driving into the deep night settles the belligerence he accumulates in the day. In the wilderness, Grandfather does not feel like the dog of a clothes-washer that belongs neither to the house nor the river-bank. Perhaps Uncle was the sneakiest, for years practicing the way to slither inside the underbelly of Africa.

Grandfather's Africa is Dodoma's orange moon, the gnarled baobab trees where spirits hang like long saliva, the yowls of hyenas, and a bottle of bundled Chivas rolling around in the trunk of his Peugeot. Around this time, I suspect, Grandmother takes her first swigs of whisky, forbidden in her religion and offensive to her values. She does it to keep him company. Grandmother is a good woman, like Sita in the *Ramayana*, like Gandhari in the *Mahabharata*, devotees of their men. One follows her husband banished to the forest. The other, upon learning from her trusted maid that she is going to be married to a blind king, commands a bandage for her eyes. She sacrifices her own sight in order to keep her husband company in his blindness. Like Sita, like Gandhari, Grandmother performs her dharma without stumbling. Grandfather, who adores his wife, does not discern the rancour in her heart.

Another Journey, Another Reincarnation

Father comes to Dodoma to die. I am almost eight, my brother five.

He is lying on a mattress at the back of a big car that has only two seats. He is holding a tattered paperback across his face. The cover is black and white, but we are too far away to see its picture. We will not get closer, not until permission is given. My brother does not remember Mother. I tell him to stop pretending. I know he has not forgotten her.

Father is given Uncle's room because it is dark and quiet. His night table has small bottles of holy water on it. Rosaries rolled like mosquito coils are everywhere. Evenings are quiet. Visitors come to see him. Even Mama Zu-zu. She opens her palm to show me a cockroach.

A witch doctor tells Grandmother if Father drinks my brother's urine, it might save him. The sores in her mouth are nubby, and so Mzee Mamudu gives her his creamy pudding, not his usual spicy fare. Father refuses the witch doctor.

Father whispers to Grandmother that after he dies, Lakshmi of Fortune will set up shop on top of the mill and lavish it with wealth. To my shoulder-boulder mother he says he wants to go. He does not feel the need to embellish. As if a strong one does not need another shoulder. He tells her she will endure (what of her ripened curves, her mass of podgy, soft skin?)

Twelve years of marriage, three gone in sickness.

One of our neighbours ties white threads on our wrists before Father is taken to the cemetery. She tells us to say goodbye, pushing our heads together so Brother and I are staring into Father's face, like at the Nairobi cancer hospital. But he is a dead stranger on the floor of our grandparents' living room, like a long plank of wood draped in white. His nostrils are plugged with cotton wool.

The mourners have arrived. The house reeks of incense. Grandmother is wearing a sweater. She is very cold. I cannot remember where Mother is. We hear hymns soft as muslin and gulps of sobs. Glasses of water make their rounds, women's faces without lipstick, our uncombed hair. We move between this room and the kitchen steps where Mzee Mamudu sits.

"Go inside a while. Then come back," he tells us. He means we should sit by our father. Neither of us cries. Adults kiss us or smooth our hair. We cut the threads off our wrists. No one notices. The threads are supposed to be on our wrists until they come off on their own.

Mother has nightmares of rushing to the Dodoma post office, trying to yank Father through the phone lines. She hears him through the mish-mash of wires, his deep voice unperturbed.

Daily, she slips out information: "Your father had a gritty voice with the warmth of ripened mangoes on top."

Mother cannot bear purple Kilimanjaro matchboxes because Father used them as tiny drums when he sang. But my brother and I never heard Father sing. We saw him at night after he closed the shop. When we saw him around the house, he was already ill.

A couple of months after Father's death, Mother tells me that she cut up her white engagement dress from neck to hem before she was married. She said she always knew she would be a widow. I think of Mr. Rochester's mad wife locked up in the tower and have nightmares of Mother coming into my room in a white gown, her raised hand carrying a butcher's knife.

Father was right. After he dies, Lakshmi plunks on top of the mill, fortune pouring out of her palms. Government contracts spill in. Our lorries, once again, revving to push off. First things first, Grandmother's secret transactions with the Sonara resume on hot and boring Dodoma afternoons. Refreshments of mangoes, salty jamuns, and treats from the Maharaja Hotel are arranged on brown windmill plates for Grandmother's loyal friend. Gold exchanged for Kenyan shillings and British sterling find their way quietly into her steel cupboard behind her long dresses wrapped in silk squares, three knots on the top, Shiva's middle eye protecting the dwellers of the house. She executes this back door task without triumph, quietly as a thief.

At thirty-four, Mother is a widow. The thought of us returning to Tukuyu is never raised. Mother is not a shopkeeper. She takes a typing course a week after Father is buried. She still wears millefleurs cotton dresses, her smile collected, but Mother herself has deserted.

Grandmother tells the Sonara, "Who is my daughter kidding?"

Mother quits typing two weeks later.

My enormous relief is her ticklish breath against my palm when she is asleep. In adulthood, the habit of checking whether Mother is dead or alive will transfer to stoves. Before I leave the house, I will check and recheck the stove a minimum of four-five-six times.

The ground is no longer steady beneath Grandfather's feet. His son is with his other mother. Tanzania is thinning of Asians. The Bhajajs are long gone. Kartar Singh is a cook in a fish and chip shop in Birmingham. Now, we are beginning to learn the names of places in England. The whole of England is no longer one big London. We are bewildered as well. Sikhs are farmers and builders. Who heard of a Sikh with pots and pans around his girth like a woman? Mzee Mamudu, upon hearing this, lets out shrill laughs. Under her breath, Grandmother says, "Hyena." Mzee Mamudu hears her all right.

"Mama, your words are only noise. Sticks and stones are breaking Indians' bones."

For a change, Grandfather takes us out to the forest during the daytime, not at night. We picnic at Cheka Cheka Creek, the laughing creek. The water is soggy with red sand. It was never a ha-ha creek. Grandfather tells us a story: a long, long time ago, an elephant came to drink water here, at Cheka Cheka, and got stuck in the mud, and that is how the town of Dodoma came to be. Walking along the pebbly path to the creek, I want to clutch Tanzania. Hold it tight. (The stones, the morass of mud, the creek's endearing name.) Kiss Koti on the mouth. I stop myself. Am I going fruity bye-bye like Mama Zu-zu? Or dorky like Grandfather? How can I forget the mill worker who pinched my nipple, still a nubby but-ton? He is still at the mill and watches me. Grandmother has two training bras wrapped in tissue, from Nairobi, ready for me in her almari. I avoid looking at them.

Last time, Mrs. Bhajaj brought us to Cheka Cheka Creek. There was me, my brother, Koti, and Jena Bai. Returning home from Cheka Cheka, we saw five policemen on the road with old, heavy pangas, museum weapons from the Maji Maji Rebellion, or from a chief's stashed loot. We knew something was wrong. Still Mrs. Bhajaj slowed down, hypnotized, like when a fire is whooshing towards you but you are stuck on the spot. Jena Bai's "Bismillah, Bismillah" whispers turned to shrieks: "Where are their cars? They are no po-licemen!" Mrs. Bhajaj told us, "Hold tight!" and stepped on the gas. We flew over potholes like Shankland. A little way off, she got out and screamed at them, "Go fuck your mothers!"

Father's pressed clothes are still in the closet. Mother stands in front of them. As if he is coming out of the shower, she is ready to lay them on the bed. But she has stopped going to the cemetery.

When Father was dying, she dreamed she was in a cemetery. After Father died, Mother regularly went to the cemetery to com-plete the forty-day ritual of pouring water on the grave. On the forty-first day, she hesitated to ask Grandfather for a lift. A widow, grown prickly, she did not want to burden her family. Kartar Singh drove her there. He waited outside. Mother tells me that everything was still, not a sound from the birds, like when a crocodile is about to attack. She understood her husband did not want her. He was dead.

Mother sleeps long hours, the itchy grey blanket (the only kind sold in Tanzania now) over her head. Grandmother fixes a cotton sheet underneath, but Mother kicks it to the floor. She wakes up with blotches all over.

The three of us, Mother, Brother, and I, sleep in the big bed by the wall in one of the middle rooms. It is strange to see Grandmother's bedroom door closed at night, as if our grandparents are guests in their horseshoe house. In the morning, Mother watches my brother and I drop prayers into our cupped palms. The rest of the day, we are the charges of our grandparents and Mzee Mamudu. My brother attaches himself firmly to the small of my back. One early morning, the sky still the colour of camp smoke, Mother hears a sharp fissure in the wall by our bed. She leaps to the veranda, grabbing both of us under her arms. From that day on, Mother quits staring at her palms. She accepts she is not meant to have ethereal collarbones looked after by a towering husband. That day, I become my mother's daughter.

In 1969, Mother applies for a matron's post in the capital, Dar es Salaam, and makes Grandfather unhappy for the second time in her life. Even as she posts the application, she knows the job is hers. In a dream, she saw a crow scoop her up and put her on the top of a huge building.

The grey hostel Mother saw in her dream has a flat at one end, our home for the next seven years. Grandfather asks Mother how she could she leave with her husband still fresh in his grave. Mother is acerbic. "It is coming close to two years since I buried him, Father."

In Dar es Salaam, Mother lets me wear rose milk lotion to school. The coastal city is so humid that baby powder turns green under our white school shirts.

Shortly after we arrive, there is another death. A boy from my new school dies. A driver knocks him off his bike and the boy flies across the road and dies on impact. I had seen him a couple of times at recess buying oranges from the hawkers like the rest of us, an ordinary boy who parted his hair on the side like other boys.

I attend the funeral. After her son is buried, when the mourners gather at her home for the traditional meal of rice and lentils, the mother serves each one personally as she whispers, "God is great." I had beseeched Allah for a miracle, leaving the Mighty One room for only a green check mark. Father died anyway. This young boy's mother is ingratiating, sucking up to Allah. She does not want Him to take her other son as well.

Every week, Mother takes us to Here-Is-Here Bookstore on Independence Avenue. When she heard its name, she said, "What a name for a bookstore, when books are supposed to take you to faraway places." I hunker down and read of heroes and battles. My favourite bedtime story is of children whose sociable fingers create rabbits and beaks on lamp-lit walls, and are stout-hearted in getting rid of the nasties. When the children put a hex on a monster, they call upon other children from all over the kingdom. Armies of children form quadruple sets of fingers, moving their mouths and fingers with speedy expertise to banish the fiend, forever. My fiend is Grandfather's enemy, Shopkeeper-with-Red-Lips. When I am older, I too will slap his face. Give him good ones across his buttocks with a kiboko. Make him eat shit. And pledges on the page, thick as treacle, move me. A citizen cries out, "Take my liver to replace my king's." His king is dying of cancer. I do not roll up my eyes in embarrassment. Or, when I read of a key under a mat, I picture a linen-yellow cottage with a puffy roof stung by bees. Kiss-curl vines speckled with oblong, orange flowers tumble down its walls. The exact moment the hero spots the heroine for the first time is when the sun casts a filigree of flowers on her cheek. Stories sustain me.

By the time we settle in the capital, Tanzania has totally segued into Mao's China. Chinese engineers, uniformly in black trousers and white shirts, are here to build roads and dams, and introduce Tanzanians to one brand of soap. At the hostel, instead of butter, slabs of Red Rose margarine are put on tables. Instead of Cornish pasty on Thursday nights, we have yam and banana stew. On other nights, it is cassava, another African dish. I chew slowly, otherwise it gets stuck in my chest. Jello and custard powder, along with other imported items like hair conditioners and peanut butter, are no longer available.

However, a strange, breezy revolution is taking over the capital, nothing to do with Mao-with-the-meaty-beauty-spot. Most youngsters say just "Dar," not "Dar es Salaam." Mercedes Benz is Merc. We pick up fashion tips from Nairobi. You can buy platforms on the black market. Mine are directly from London. Grandfather brought them back for me, light blue with a streak of yellow. (When Grandfather and Grandmother holiday in London, Grandfather will not stop over in Dar es Salaam. Mother does not beseech him like my brother and I.) I wobble in my platforms on the potholed roads of Upanga, the area we live in. I wear Koti's purple socks to school (that he gave to me when I left Dodoma).

Indian girls are placed in military service, mandatory after Form VI. They return toughened, slurping sweet tea and polishing off thick slices of white bread spread with Red Rose margarine. Even Indian film stars, put up at the Hotel Kilimanjaro, have short, swishy hair, the long, demure plait chopped off. The girls at the hostel where we live like disco. I am one of them. We all dig James Brown. When we hear "I Feel Good," we jump up to dance on the common room floor. In Dar es Salaam, hostel girls are known to be good dancers, and we show off our skills at dance performances, parties, and social functions.

For the first time, not a film actress but a real Indian-Tanzanian like me is my heroine. Amal Kara. The first time I see her is at Paradise Cinema. She is holding hands with a black Tanzanian.

Swankers from the University of Dar es Salaam, Indian and African students, saunter into the Paradise Cinema like they own the place to watch films like *Guess Who's Coming to Dinner?* I miss Koti. When I watch *To Sir, with Love*, about a disruptive class that gets a new teacher, I imagine Koti and me as the surly teenagers in the teacher's class.

Grandfather sees *To Sir* as well, at Ramson's Cinema, and likes Lulu who sings the theme song and also stars in the film. In the film, with her snub nose and shaggy haircut, she is second best, more personality than looks. She is the pretty heroine's best friend. Lulu is the shoulder-boulder kind who manages things like Mother. Grandfather and I like her more than the sappy heroine. He says she is nothing like the British memsahibs of Africa with whalebone crimpers for smiles.

I write to Koti, c/o P.O. Box 11, to tell him about the film. He writes back that he was in Moshi with Uncle Chando for a holiday, but tells me that Don Black wrote the lyrics (a new word for me) to the song and Mark London composed the music. I thought singers wrote their own songs. He also writes a joke that only I understand. Thailand is thigh-land and Lulu is a tsetse. Nothing to do with the terrifying brown fly, its long probes digging into the backs of animals and humans, making them die of sleeping sickness. Lulu is a tsetse means Lulu is a sexy. He has seen her photographs in *Good Housekeeping*, which Uncle Chando subscribes to.

The tail end of the decade is a mish-mash of Nyerere's rose-coloured Tanzania, of going back to villages, and of sharing property. Heady times. The list of razzmatazz swankers: James Brown, Sidney Poitier, and Amal Kara. And platforms, Afros, headbands (I make good use of Grandfather's imported ties from Gentlemen's Court on Bond Street), and purple socks.

It is in Dar es Salaam that I see the spiny line—like the woman's in Uncle's magazine—between my own new breasts. And feel the spurt of warm wetness.

Then there is the beginning of the exodus: the number of Indians leaving East Africa swells overnight. In 1972, burly and demented Idi Amin of neighbouring Uganda wants Ugandan-Indians out, like pronto, clear off! Mwalimu is not happy. But Indian-Tanzanians *want* out. Indians continue to leave Tanzania to settle in India, Pakistan, Portugal, Germany, the United Kingdom, America—and Canada.

Pierre Elliott Trudeau, Prime Minister of Canada, takes in planeloads of refugees from Uganda. We are enchanted by the man. None of us know what he looks like (we imagine him a tall hero), until a photograph of him appears in the *Sunday News*. We read and reread his wide, slightly jutting forehead (sign of a seer), his hot, beady eyes, his scraggy, high cheekbones (like cliffs), his small pinched mouth (a sign of determination). The Indians had started their love affair with Pierre Trudeau, from the Indian-Canuck in Canada to the cook on the Grand Trunk Road in India. We watch him: Trudeau of the red rose in the lapel of his henna-coloured trench coat. Trudeau of the collars dashed up. (Once in Canada, those of us who had not seen him in person were startled to learn he was not tall.) Before Idi Amin, Canada is in grainy black and white photographs in our geography books, a lacklustre tundra, a numbing Arctic that we bother to study only for the O-Levels. Suddenly, Indians are on a high to come to Canada. To become a toilet cleaner, a cabbie, or to join the CPR, all is good. Those who do not know what CPR stands for are defiant—who cares? It could mean 'C' for cat and 'P' for pork. What Indian motherfucker cares?

Meanwhile, Grandfather's Africa is disintegrating under his swollen, diabetic feet. He clamours for sweets. By the time he lands at the cancer hospital in Nairobi, Grandfather's Africa has crumbled completely, every Indian's feet anxiously tapping; but first, two smart slaps across an African's cheek, then jump aboard the plane.

Grandfather is diagnosed with cancer. He does not fight tooth and nail like Father. He says he is done. He is not going to leave Africa to move anywhere else.

Grandmother keeps quiet. But Mother has plans. Her dreams guided her in the past. (Before moving to the hostel in Dar es Salaam, she saw a grey building with a bird perched on top.) Now, looking out her window one night thinking of where we could go, she gets a sign. She has been thinking it would be Australia. There is a huge mango tree behind our flat. She hears the thud of a mango fall to the ground. She wakes us up. For a moment Brother and I think it is Grandfather waking us for a night ride in the forest. But Mother has sliced mangoes in a bowl. She tells us, "We are going to Canada. I think soon."

By 1975, Grandfather is in the Nairobi cancer hospital. Grandmother stays with him. Mother takes us there. Grandfather is smoking his Ten Cent cigarettes and likes nougats, Chinese ones. He appoints us to peel off the gauzy, handmade wrappings. Grandfather says I can marry Koti in a few years. Mother tells him Koti's mother is taking him to France. She tells him we are going to Canada. Grandfather tells Mother to go to hell. It is not as if they never talk again after this moment, but their communication becomes formal. He has let her go, resigned to the fact that she will do as she pleases.

When Grandfather dies, we bury him in Nairobi.

Mother starts the immigration process.

An Indian restaurateur in Calgary arranges work for her as a cook. Mother can only boil milk! She does not take lessons from Mzee Mamudu. What if the interviewer asks for a demonstration? She says she will not end up in a restaurant kitchen.

Maa is handing over the mill to Uncle Chando and the house to Mzee Mamudu.

Once again, she deals with the Sonara, this time for American dollars. This money quietly reaches Canada before we do.

*   *   *

I often wonder about those pernicious times when the Sonara came over with stronger Kenyan currency to pay for Father's hospital bills and left with Grandmother's gold. Selling her gold in secrecy, did Grandmother's long skirts rise slightly in agitation? Did she permit the Sonara to sit on her marriage bed, gold strewn between them? Did the Sonara's eyes spy her never-before-exposed ankle, virginal, one could say, out of purdah for a blink of an eye? Like a bereft woman pulling up her kurta to rub her belly in despair, Grandmother, not in her senses, might have let her long frock rise. Then did our Sonara's surreptitious eye slink onto her exquisite instep? Would he have, ever so cleverly, dabbed his senses on her forbidden throaty ankle, ravished it, with no one to know? After all, foxy lapidary that he was, even the angel perched on his right shoulder would not have been able to unconditionally nail his dirt.

But the Sonara, I want to believe, was a denizen from the golden age of Rama and Sita. Not pulpy soft as his gold, there was bamboo strength in the man's character. When some custodians arrive back door, their scruples cannot be muscled with. Our Sonara, I want to believe, was one of them.

First thing first upon arrival in Calgary, Alberta, Canada, 1976, Grandmother buys a house in Marlborough, in the northeast of the city. In Dodoma, Grandmother had the Sonara. In Calgary, she garners sparkles for her garden journal from Lessia Petriv of the Ukrainian Cultural Heritage Village:

- sprinkle Sunlight soap at the edge of gardens to keep deer away.

There are no deer in the suburbs of Marlborough.

When I learn about John Rowand in my Canadian history course at Mount Royal College, right after class I take the #110 bus to Grandmother's house in Marlborough to tell her about the obese and eccentric government official in Edmonton who used his prodigious fist to get his way. He had glass packed in barrels of molasses and shipped to him all the way from England for the windows of his three-storey house in Edmonton, the first house to have glass windows out west. What fascinates Maa is that glass was packed in molasses.

"It did not break?" she asks.

But after our conversation, she does not acknowledge or bring this man up in conversation again, just like she does not bring up Uncle, the son she gave up.

Grandfather was the Lion of Dodoma, charismatic. He pushed his weight about. Many capitulated. Like Grandfather, John Rowand of the Hudson Bay Company was a man either loved or loathed, an unpredictable grizzly. Yet his nightingale's charm could coax an ant to trail right under his boot.

I press on. I bring up Rowand with Grandmother on another day, a Sunday. We are in her bed. Calgary's winter sun streaming through her window is hot.

"Does he not remind you of someone?" I poke.

The eggy smell of breakfast has wafted to the bedroom, but Grandmother refuses to open the windows even a tad to freshen the air, just as she brushes off the similarities between Grandfather and John Rowand, both of sensuous disposition, roaring tempers, and bellicose ambitions. Grandmother's journey with Grandfather is done. Who looks back at the ferry boat from which one has disembarked? Not Grandmother. Done. Done. Done. She is on another shore, on another journey, in another reincarnation.

The Exits:

Present Day –
Flight to Calgary

Calgary, Alberta, Canada (1976–...)
Chonju, South Korea (1995–...)
Delhi, India (1982–...)

Departing

After being away from home, I crave food-food. I crave thick char-grilled tenderloin. But I cannot stride up to the Air Canada desk at Incheon International, seventy kilometres from Seoul, ask with Albertan charm, "Is there any real food on the plane?" and hear the flight attendant's long peal of laughter, her unfurling red carpet welcome. It would not come out right. My tone would be huffy, or like sudden money.

With exact measure, I fit my knapsack in the overhead compartment above my seat. I already feel two inches taller on the airplane that is taking me home to the prairies. The rows part, like the Red Sea, as I sail to my seat.

The seat belt sign has been switched off. The drink trolley is almost here. The guy next to me is ready to chat, ready for a ten-hour-floaty-closeness. But I look out the window. I am flying to the prairies. I want to be left alone.

A seasoned immigrant, I slide a door across my face and let myself go.

Dear Prairies,

Can loving you be more than an act of imagination?

Can one love a place like a lover?

Let others triumphantly wave their blue passports in the air. Peacock strutters with their First World cachet. At Stampede ethnic spreads, others grovel at the feet of red-faced officials. Let them curry favours. I am no brown-nosing Juliet. Mother never had a widow's smell, and I am not a beggar with drippy hair in a refugee line. Mine is a vainglorious mane. If you wish, meet me by a fence post, tonight.

I could call you "love," my Prairies. Sometimes I do. Most of all, you are my under-the-rose secret, my silent corridor romance. I will not prove up. I will not swoon over the wood of hockey sticks. (The game bores me.) But may I decorate your lunch box? This way, lay a claim on you at the barn dance.

Under-the-rose, a perfect name for a tryst, perfect for secrecy and confessions, like mulchy brown soil covered with woody weeds and thatch on top, so the ribby wind will not blow it away. A noble blade romance.

I met you before 1976, before Grandmother, Mother, Brother, and I arrived in Calgary. I met you in Dar es Salaam in a school text-book. You were grainy tundra photographs for an exam. You meant nothing to me except the correct answer. Then, in 1972, magic happened. Trudeau of Canada opened his third eye, and the next thing you know Ugandan Asians are flying to their new homes in Canada. The rest of us wanted the same, gaga over Trudeau. Show your bum to Idi Amin, Nyerere, and the Queen, we are off to Canada. In Dar es Salaam, I was saucy with the Canadian interviewer (grey-suited, he had pale rock star hair), already not proving up. Mother did not hush me when I told him I looked forward to peanut butter in Canada (did not know the smooth kind existed) and shampoo that made hair shine. Black market items to die for, I told him. I had not yet met the Breck Girls. Three pretty faces on a shampoo bottle, one above the other, like the steps of a staircase. Toothsome optimism in their freckled, upturned noses. The good life, for which an immigrant pulls out the gold from her teeth, crosses shark-infested waters. She will do anything for safe, orange school buses, for patio lights on green lawns, for transactions clear as a bell, and for children already born with stethoscopes around their necks. The good life. Full time.

My under-the-rose heart, I do not want that of you. Tip my chin instead. Ask me to dance.

I am waiting for you by a fence post, sometimes in Calgary but often somewhere else where your arrival is always startling as a blue sunflower. At times, the wait is unbearably long. You do not turn up. And so, bogged down with work, or preoccupied with travelling, I think I have forgotten you. I might think, I do not need you, I have had enough of you. Then I see a pair of red shorts flying on a clothesline, but in a backyard in Chonju. I catch a smell of Sunday breakfast, but out in the street, in Delhi. Something familiar made unfamiliar sharpens my hunger to be with you. I wait for you to return, to walk right into my arms.

Flying to you first time, on Air France with Grandmother, Brother, and Mother, I wore a new pink crimplene suit and, like a Bedouin, carted all the gold I could on my body. My neck and arms shining with gold. The Tanzanian government permitted us leave with $200 each, I think. I cannot remember now, but it was a paltry sum. Back then, in the 1970s, pilots walked up and down the aisles, hosts of their airplanes. Seeing the mound of gold on my body, one of them did a double take.

At Charles de Gaulle that winter morning in 1976, and even later when the immigration officer in Toronto stamped our pink papers, I was not yet in awe of Canada, nor did I have gratitude for the quietude of a second chance. Grandfather's beefy blood roiling in mine, I arrived insubordinate as an aristocrat, or, truer still, I arrived insubordinate as a lover who takes liberties. Mother, as well, arrived on her own terms. She had changed scents. From Apple Blossom to the dashed-up collar chic of Bond Street. She had done it before, choosing a path and not looking back. She married a man of whom her father disapproved; in secret she applied for a post in Dar es Salaam; and now she was helping herself to a honey pour in Canada. Yes, Mother set things in motion. She was not going to step inside the laundry room at The Four Seasons to wash semen off guests' sheets for the fabled Canadian job experience. In two days, she would land a clerical job, teach herself to type, and eventually move up to the post of an administrative assistant in a big insurance office downtown Calgary.

A young woman who had been on the flight to Paris with us had trouble getting on the escalator. She toppled getting off. I was not going to be her, starting from scratch, just like Mother knew she was not going to be a cook in Canada. I saw a tall French woman in a poncho and shiny jackboots pushing one of the glass doors open with her shoulder. She had coffee and round bread in her hands. Her hair was not elderly grey, but platinum, shimmering warmly like pelt. Watching her swing through the doors, two chic braids down her hips, I decided I would love you, my Prairies, like a lover.

> There are elephants on the prairies
> in a tender-foot getup.
> Do your ears prick up?
> > Girth and a quick step,
> > girth and a quick step,
> left my earring, search for my earring,
> on the prairies, the prairies.
>
> I say sunflowers, you say spits.
> I say barn dance, you say barn up.
> I am here today, gone tomorrow,
> the constant of exits my permanent address.
> Will you send me a love note back?

Almost Bridal

First time Brother and I saw red grain elevators, they reminded us of Grandparents' entrance door. In the back seat of Stranger-Uncle's car, we had been solemn children from Tukuyu to Dodoma. But after all the flying from Dar es Salaam to Vancouver, finally zipping along a zany-wide prairie highway, we kept swallowing like we were still in the air, our ears plugged up.

"Enormous!" I said, pointing at a grain elevator wheezing by.

"Gynormous!" my brother responded.

This time, we did not have phone numbers to learn by heart. Mother's face had not gone away. She intently watched the speeding scenery. When I asked my brother whether grain elevators stored secrets, I was thinking of Grandmother who had stored hers with sober wariness. My brother shrugged and slid back to his window. He did not want to be bothered with that anymore. An immigrant's whining and sob story eyes exasperated him even then, newly arrived himself and only a child.

"Time to get off the damn boat!" became his response.

But for me: Taber corn, the auctioneer at the corral, the whiff of slightly pissy soup on a back stove, or snug announcements

SHEEP CREEK WEAVERS AND QUILTERS

IN

OLD ICE CREAM BUILDING

felt awesomely distant, almost bridal, like when I was nine and one of my aunts in Dodoma got engaged. She was not our funny aunt anymore, the aunt who squeezed my brother and me so tight, then asked, "Did your poo come out?" The morning after her engagement she was already out of reach as she crossed the veranda in her familiar grey nightie to go to the toilet. At the washbasin, she swished her hair over the other side of her face. It was an action apart from the rest of us, exotic.

Once, my friend, who sleeps with her windows slightly open even in Calgary's bitter-cold February, brought me six perfect peaches in a painted box from 17th Avenue. If I am going away, she brings me purple sage from the outskirts of the city ("to remind you of home," she says). I roll the sage in my underwear and inhale its fragrance when I leave it to dry in a drawer elsewhere, in another country. When I am in town, often we go to Millarville Farmers' Market on basky Saturday summer mornings, a fifty-minute drive out of Calgary. My friend drives a convertible. She says you are allowed to wave when you are in a convertible. Is that not simply Zen-Chinook?

On the prairies, the moon is not a witch doctor's orange. At the peak of summer, Calgary's moon above Nose Hill Park races alongside my bus as we head north on John Laurie Boulevard, towards my home. You can tell it is the bus driver's final trip for the day, for he is driving jauntily and cannot help the grin on his face. Some years ago, Mother and Brother bought a house close to Nose Hill Park and the YMCA. Brother, like me, has no predilection for marriage. I spend summers with Mother and Brother. The moon outside my bus window, story-book wide. When the dainty, blue truck packed with Taber corn is parked behind the Y at the corner of Nose Hill and John Laurie, and flowers have sudden eye makeup, and the strawberry-orange moon on Nose Hill hammocks or races as it pleases, it is a summer night in Calgary. When Brother's barbeque chicken marinates in garlic and cilantro, and Calgary is giddy with the off-the-shoulder pleasure of smoky lotion, it is a summer evening on the prairies.

In Tukuyu, besides our grandparents' address, Mother taught us both to look at our hands upon waking up.

"This way," she said, "you catch the first happy thoughts of the day."

The childhood habit of gazing into his cupped palms has lingered with my brother. Early mornings in Calgary, his penchant for car exotica plops straight from his mouth and shimmers in his palms.

"I have installed the beefy parts of the racing engine, but the girly parts are so darn expensive," he tells us one morning at breakfast. He watches Mother closely. Mother continues to eat her Weetabix. "Nothing?" he asks her, exasperated.

Mother shakes her head.

He is always hoping that she will throw him a bone when it comes to scrumptious motorcar paraphernalia, she, who can read the future in a dream, or make sense of a sign. Brother longs for Mother to tell him his fortunes are just around the corner, that he, after all, will be successful in building his dream car. The dream car that Brother and his best friend spend every moment on. Brother's dream car in the garage, literally guzzling his money, with parts imported from the States and Germany. Any sign.

One summer morning, Mother and I were walking home after a workout at the Y, cutting across the fields, and she felt the graze of someone's jacket.

"Allah be with you," she whispered.

"Did you feel a spirit?"

"I think so. He wore a sky blue bomber jacket. Can you smell animal fat in the air?" she asked.

Even though neither my brother nor I have the stomach for scary movies, let alone thrillers, when Mother is beside me I am not scared.

"Was he agitated like the spirits at the cemetery in Dodoma?"

"No, he knew where he was going. Our paths crossed, that is all."

"Did you see his back, was it scooped out? Could you see inside his body? Did he walk pigeon-toed?"

Mother's face became distant.

"OK. I will not poke."

"Do not tell your brother. I do not want him alarmed."

As simple as the fact that I will always be eldest, I will always do anything to guard him. Even in adulthood. I love him.

In addition to the signs and spirits she encounters on walks, from her bedroom window Mother spends a lot of time simply watching the moon. At breakfast, one meal Mother insists we eat together, my brother often teases her.

"So Mother, where did you fly out last night?"

According to her, she did "fly out" a couple of times early on when we first came to Canada, and calmly reported it to us at breakfast the next day. Each time my brother got more and more spooked, so she eventually stopped. Now when she watches the moon intently he tells her to cut it out. However, he listens to her advice, what she can foresee, especially when it comes to investments or changing jobs. Although she has never been able to predict anything about his beloved cars.

Still, my brother's transition to Canada has been happy gulps of air. Prayers fall into his cupped hands here as they did in Africa. A middle of the road guy, who prefers a barber to a hairstylist, he is unable to understand that buying in bulk soothes Mother. Mother always has at least three bottles of Harveys Bristol Cream in the pantry. My brother often asks her when the liquor store became another Costco. Never to run out of stock is her sanctuary: in anticipation of the Sunday pleasure of the whole family watching *60 Minutes* together, a bowl of sherry trifle chilling in the fridge, she hoards supplies.

I like to do the family's grocery shopping. Usually, my brother drops me off on his way to work. After reading the *Globe and Mail* with my coffee, I leisurely fill my cart. The aisles are mostly empty. Shopping done, I ring Associated Cabs to pick me up in twenty-five minutes. Another coffee in hand, I wait outside.

I do not let go of warm winter boots in May, not even in June, but I enjoy the sting of the cold on my bare cheeks. One day, waiting for my cab, I watch an old couple stop outside so that the man can button his wife's coat. He does not chide her for not buttoning up inside. His wife turns her head sideways to give his shaky, gnarled fingers room. Mother does not have a widow's smell, but still never will experience the tenderness of a husband buttoning her coat when she needs help. Grandfather called Grandmother his love till the day he died at the Nairobi cancer hospital. I have read that when a moose calls for his beloved, it stirs up a man's liver.

I daydream of a man dressed in furs (tu, tu, tu) coming to rescue me in a winter storm. I tear my petticoat into strips for napkins, placing them by two big bowls I use for making bread. I live with him in his cabin, forever.

But wearing a beaver's pelt requires an innate ease that cannot be feigned. How would I look? Probably, like an over-lipsticked ar-riviste. Grandfather was already a grandee. Had he come over, he would have worn pelt svelte, without a second thought. Once I did ask Grandmother if she ever thought of ordering a beaver pelt for Grandfather from ways-a-way Canada.

"I thought Canada was the North Pole. Who shops there?"

Yes, *where is Canada?* An overdone question, yet a Gordian knot. At school in Dar es Salaam, Canada was the forsaken tundra, until the blast from Trudeau's eye. Usually, from here to Timbuktu, everyone yawps of Canada's goodness, and then the ice cream freeze: *where is Canada?* Or a person may rearrange it like living room furniture. A middle-aged woman in Los Angeles foursquarely told me she had been to Canada in Montreal. Canada surrounded by the country of Montreal, sidewalk cafés and women draped in throw-on shawls.

But I do not believe I have the cheek to step inside a fur shop to feel a beaver's pelt. It would be like changing my name to fit in— although I do filch details my friends mention, like beaver pelt is ten times softer than pashmina.

Even in thready sneakers, Canadians fly across icy crosswalks. Legs bent, gusty winds smacking against their smartly extruded tor-sos, they sagaciously cut across the slippery terrain. Snippets of hair outside their knitted caps are cold and alive. Their strong, yellow teeth shine with glee.

The old couple walks to their car. I follow the woman's plum red coat, plum, plum, and spot a middle-aged immigrant standing on an icy patch, also in the parking lot. The difference between them is evident. The couple knows how to tread snow. Snow has been in the thickness of their wrists and ankles for generations, but the middle-aged immigrant is petrified. It does not occur to him to find a clearer path to the store, or perhaps it is his private conversion that will not let him.

The moment is quiet. No official or judge will witness this singular moment. He has left behind property, degradation, and death. He rises from his plane seat, ready to prove up, this way kiss the ground. To find a way around the icy patch would be deception. He could not be a pioneer who erected a house with his own bare hands. At least he could manage an icy path. He is stern with other pleasures as well, like reading the paper from the beginning to the end instead of diving to the business section first. That would be like cutting in front of someone. He is so capable. But that was in Tanzania. Here, in an icy parking lot, the immigrant feels the mad glitter of ice ready to split his bones to hair.

Revving to leave Africa, he must have told the Canadian officer, flown from Toronto to Dar es Salaam, even impatiently, "God has given me teeth, I know I will chew." There would have been no apprehension about success once he entered the country, nor, for that matter, snow. Snow was like sand, only cold, no? Now its validity hangs about him like a noose all year round. The immigrant shudders. How can he glide on ice with the nonchalance of a polar bear? He does not have Canadian feet.

"I have two left feet," he tells the woman who comes to his rescue, then gets red in the face. He has used the wrong phrase. She is not asking him to dance.

Inside his skin, the immigrant's English is impatient, unedited. He is not the organized kind to check things off a list. Everything in his head is brightly stored. His brain is no dumb coconut, and this head-eating disease of making lists with sharp, yellow pencils by the phone in the new country is worse than a nagging wife. But when he hears himself aloud, guttural, blubbering phrases, and feels the woman's kind hand under his elbow, he shrinks, already an old man.

I could not have endured Grandfather's vapidity in Canada, a new country to him, watching his shoulders slop girlish, and his sweater flop about him like Mama Titi's loose yams. What if he could not have been a grandee here and power turned funny on him? I have seen such men at the checkout counters, their sweaters hanging string-bag loose. They are touchy with requests. They think they will not be heard.

I turn away. This man must not see me. There is no calamity more painful than another immigrant observing your cap-in-hand misery. He does not know I have snow fright as well and do not drive in winter. Our weatherman's conviviality already clearing yesterday's thirty-centimetre pileup. His disarming dimples coaxing Calgarians to shake off the grumps: only ten centimetres this morning!

What terrifies me the most is the indifference of the direction-less snow. It has no mouth or bowels. And it is soundless. There is no second chance.

When living in Dodoma, when my brother and I missed Mother, especially after she rang from the cancer hospital in Nairobi in her wishy-washy voice, Mzee Mamudu would tell us the story about the mother washing clothes on the beach. Hands on his knees, supper of red kidney beans bubbling on the stove, he would narrate:

> The clothes she had wrung dry began to grow eyes. They stung like pellets on her shins: go now, go now! The mother leapt across the air and plunged into the water to tear her son out of a crocodile's jaws, by the skin of her teeth, as the expression goes.

We were consoled. Mother would always come back when it was time to save us. Then we would be off to Tukuyu, back home.

But what is the Canadian story of saving oneself, of survival? Of a hunter so cold that he slashes the belly of a moose to plunge his frozen hands into its steamy blood for heat? This is a scary flick. Snow without a mouth or bowels and utterly quiet is too nerve-jangling for a Canuck from Tanzania.

But I want to be replete with snow. I do, like the old couple driving away. When will I dream in flannel?

I spend a languid winter afternoon in Grandmother's big bed before I ready for a journey abroad. For now, savoury beef in the oven, infusing the house.

Grandmother, in her late eighties, is hell-bent on matching black underwear from Victoria's Secret.

"In Dodoma, women sought to enchant even as they slept," she says. I remember the spread of her long nightdress that she wore in Dodoma. It sharpened her dainty top waistline.

"Not Mother, she did not sleep dressily in bed." I say.

"No, your mother did not have a chance, worried sick about your father. Ten years of marriage, you are still wet behind the ears, coping to be a wife. In a panic, your mother cut up her engagement dress, you know that? We had to have another one made for the engagement ceremony in a hurry, an ivory-coloured shift with lace at the neck and sleeves. The tailor could not do anything more elaborate, not within the twenty-four hours I gave her. If your mother knew she would end up a widow, why did she marry him?"

"Even she does not know."

"She told you that?"

"In passing."

"Of course, your mother's way with calamity is dropping the shocker on the way to the bathroom."

"Maybe she did not want to inconvenience anyone."

"You mean she did not want to inconvenience your father. He was not even her husband then!"

"Maa, you loved Father!"

"Yes, but I would have fought tooth and nail if I knew he would make her a widow. I taught her only too well to first check whether the men have had enough to eat, enough space in the closet, and more than enough happiness coming out their ears."

I have wondered, often, if Grandmother would be able to consider, can a country be one's lover? Would she understand that after a decade in Calgary I must fly away, for work, in search of new opportunity—but that after every decision to leave the country I become discombobulated. I start paying attention to the insignificant, like a roll of toilet paper secured with a bit of brown tape so it will not unfurl, or the spot on my yo where I spilt coffee that reminds me of maraschino cherries in the fridge (Mother does not bake, so I always make cherry squares first thing when I am back home). Journeys bring out the inconsequential. Love is garnered in what is not ordinarily noticed.

Since coming to Canada, Grandmother has risen out of the ashes. She shines with what she calls "luminous intention."

"Luminous intention, that is fanciful diamond talk," I tell her.

"Are not diamonds mined up north, here?"

"Yes, of course."

"So … would you rather I talk like I am obsessed with the weather, turning to the weather channel all the time?"

"No, Maa."

Loving you, my under-the-rose heart, sometimes the language is glittery like Maa's. Plain no-nonsense English does not cut it. It is candy. When speaking in this language, there are friendly winks from a ship-shape house jinni with a svelte showbiz stomach. Buying chocolate muscles from a love shop, housewives giggle, their hair pulled back in ponytails. The language has a feel, a good pace. Everyone drops years conversing in it.

But even thoroughly suffused in this language, one cannot help notice what is seen, quite visible, but not addressed: a widow's leg, once plump and young, now wrinkling with age as she carefully climbs out of the bathtub. This arouses the sensation of the sting, the sock to the mouth, that anything may be taken away. Even a walk around the neighbourhood causes fear and pain.

Still, the mellow lights in Grandmother's living room have a persimmon's glow. I think of pudding, the loveliest treat at the end of a meal, when everything has the curve of tulips and the softness of earlobes. Puddings assert home. Sweet reckonings of cake soaked in sherry and custard, good night, sleep tight.

"Here I am free. I can live by my own intentions. Back in Do-doma," Grandmother says, "I was always steadying what Grand-father toppled, cleaning his dump with an invisible toilet brush. Your grandfather had bright ideas but not genuine ones. As if others in Dodoma had no conviction.

"Your grandfather always rocked the boat, rock, rock, rock, and I had to steady it each time and placate everyone. I dared not budge from his side. One day, the walls began to close in on me with the gloat of a second wife. That is how it got.

"He loved me and I lived for him. That was the way. But here, I am my own hyena in petticoats."

She means Nellie McClung, a thorn in the hide of the politician who liked gentle women who fetched his papers and slippers and brought him hot milk in bed. He called her a hyena in petticoats.

"That Nellie would have set your grandfather straight. Pick up a toilet brush. Clean up your damn mess."

"Maa, until the end he serenaded you."

"He was serenading himself."

In Dodoma, I cannot help but think Maa would have lumped Nellie McClung with the Tall Woman and the obdurate Amba hounding Bhisma even in death. But in Canada, Nellie is like her best friend. The only thing she insists on now is that I scrape snow off my shoes before I come indoors.

"This land is a diamond. It has given me a second chance."

"Maa. You embellish."

"Child, what else do you embellish with if not diamonds?"

Connecting

We have landed at Vancouver International. At gate B11, from where my flight departs for Calgary, a clean-cut Albertan is helping middle-aged Japanese tourists whose boarding cards, handed out at Narita, are screwed up. The heavy-set Air Canada ground employee with un-scrunched hair, solidly fifty-plus, wants to know exactly who is getting on *her* plane. Damn if a plane will be hijacked from under her nose. Her territorial claim makes me want to snap up things with the intense acquisitive nature of a bony spinster. I am not that! I have a vainglorious mane of hair. Even with such sensual heft, I am unable to shake off the shoddy baggage tied with silly ropes, formerly plunked on top of Dodoma's tumbledown buses alongside chicken coops and carsick goats.

The Albertan suddenly becomes an attaché. The Japanese flock around him. He bows. I bet he only speaks grocery store Japanese.

- Mushrooms, please.
- Soap, please.

But at B11, his language skills knock off socks. The Japanese careen necks and ogle at the superstar dispensing information, quietly organizing their boarding cards as he confers with the tough Air Canada worker. True, with an Albertan about you do not have to wait long. Five Albertans will jump out of five separate cars when yours gets stuck in snow. The young Albertan's dash is even more exquisite because of the solid gold band on his ring finger. There is nothing newfangled about him. He is downright homegrown.

And he does not exude sudden money in his tone. In his place, an immigrant's accent may be too decorative, gobbets of dusty English locked in a colonial go-down from somewhere, peremptory with commandments. In Tanzania, when an order is issued by the big bwana, a fleet of serfs carries it out. But in Canada, the boss also has to unpack boxes. So sometimes an educated immigrant's scabrous tone is reserved for fellow immigrants.

One time, an Indian pharmacist escorted Mother to the right shelf. Being from the culture where respect for elders is in demonstration, he felt obliged to escort her to the shelf himself, then his tone turned accusatory.

"The drops are right here!"

"Translated," Mother said, "means you have potatoes for eyes!"

From a lonely spot in the corridor, I watch the Albertan's never-locked hospitality of "Come on over!" The pharmacist who helped Mother could not help himself. The Albertan, so back-pocket-casual courteous; but for the pharmacist, the mish of new and the mash of old turned funny on him.

My Prairies, My Dear Under-the-Rose,

Something new: the prairies.

Something old: the silk squares Grandmother folds her dresses in.

Scarves, bandages, diapers, and petticoats are my arousals. I hear sugar sacks can make excellent diapers. That flour sacks can be sewn into a man's shirt. But I would not know a feed sack if I saw one.

In a pioneer woman's hands, feed sacks became tea towels, shirts, and underwear. A century ago, kitchens had a tin of Diamond Dyes that could dye anything from feathers to stockings, their advertisement claimed. Some women swore by Fels-Naptha or Sunlight with salt to remove the stubborn green and brown image of a Robin Hood with his arrow drawn, though the smirking hero never completely faded. Feed bags for salt and small cereal were pocket-sized, the size appealing, like a sonara's fuchsia wrapping papers for jewels.

Do you know of Gandhari from the *Mahabharata*? The would-be queen who told her maid to blindfold her before she married the blind king? But in her old age, she also told her, with bitterness, that not once had the king asked her to remove the bandages from her eyes. But Grandmother did. In Canada, she did away with her bandages and the glut of wifely dharma.

In Chonju, I once heard a story, an old story, of a nobleman's daughter who, when she was fifteen, draped her petticoat over the coffin of a shoemaker. He had once come to her house to measure her feet.

When the procession of mourners passed the gates of the nobleman's house, the coffin sank its weight deep into the shoulders of the pallbearers, refusing to budge until the broken-hearted mother of the dead shoemaker revealed what had happened. She confessed that her son had fallen in love with the nobleman's daughter when he came to measure her feet. He knew he could never marry her, their stations distinct as reincarnations, and "My son," the mother wept, "died of a broken heart."

In front of the rest of the mourners, the nobleman's daughter lifted her skirts to remove her white petticoat. She draped it over the young shoemaker's coffin. She remembered snippets of the day she laid eyes on him, her maid behind her, giggling. Both of them amused by the shoemaker's cheeks, flushed, like red peppers. She absorbed dully what the mourners told her: that he was still an apprentice, not even a fully-fledged shoemaker.

That night, the nobleman's daughter swore to a huge orange moon that by publicly removing her petticoat for the shoemaker she had declared her heart. Henceforth, she was beholden to no man. There was one and he had died. The nobleman's daughter left her father's home to become a famous kisaeng, who entertained nobility with dance and searing poetry.

Grandfather stepped out of the steamy bathroom, blots of pink prayer ribboning off his skin cleansed with Lifebuoy soap. Maa tied the top of her bundles with three knots, the middle one being Shiva's eye, protecting the spaces in cupboards. The Sonara's magic came from his instep, his feet barely touched the ground. And my arousals are scarves, bandages, diapers, and petticoats. Sometimes I tell friends, when I am away, "I best be getting home, his eyes will be watching the gate." I mean you, my Prairies, waiting for me with Goody hairgrips wrapped in flannel.

> If you happened to see a pair of earrings left by a
>   broken-hearted lover,
> would you sob and sob for her?
> Would you, my under-the-rose heart?
> Would you holler at God, waving your steaming blue
>   liver in His face?
>
> My earrings are puffy umbrellas.
> Find them for me.
>
>   Girth and a quick step,
>   girth and a quick step,
> left my earring, search for my earring,
>   on the prairies, the prairies.

Away From Home, An Upright Place

My apartment in Chonju is dilapidated, like the rest of the building. The water is orange, and we go to work with orange stains on
our clothes. Most teachers in the building are from North America,
a few from Japan, France, and Germany. And there is a Spanish
teacher who holds onto plastic bags, an Everest of plastic bags in her
apartment.

The apartment building is at one end of the campus of Chonbuk National University, where I teach in the Language Education
Center. I stay out of the apartment as much as possible. The building,
surrounded by trees and wild greenery, has a nearby pond, similar
to ones in calendars with Korean country scenery. Frogs croak in the
pond after a downpour, under a full moon creamy as cheese, and a
good time to sip beer by the pond is late afternoon. Or, after 6 p.m.,
I hang out with the other teachers at Chonju Coffee House or we
meet at Dandelion for gin and tonics. The Stable Rooted Tree, my
regular teahouse, is my second home. Sometimes, my more petrified
students write their exams at the Tree. Folk music, incense, and the
oval stone pond with itty-bitty orange fish darting here and there
calm their jitters.

The only couple in our building have a slow cooker and, to the
rest of us, this is an exotic item.

One of the teachers makes her own lasagna noodles. She hangs
them over chairs to dry. We all bring our chairs over to her apartment for noodle hanging.

In 1995, cheese can be purchased readily in Seoul, four hours
away by bus, but in Chonju it is exorbitantly expensive.

Texas Billy lives in 047 (and I in 048). We co-teach a few courses, share sweet basil, unavailable in Chonju, that his mother sends him from San Antonio, and split beers at 3 x 3, our regular bar. The woman he is crazy about spends weekends at his place. One night, after a couple of beers, Billy asks me if I have ever heard them knocking boots.

"You mean, did I hear you?"

"Did you?"

"No." A lie. The walls are paper-thin.

Away from home, I have always managed an upright place. I am differently tidy. No empty shampoo or lotion bottles in the bathroom. Just about every day I lift the sticky lid of the recycling bin buzzing with summer flies to dump out empty stubby stout bottles. Korea's dark lager, chilled stout, is the new rage in bars. In our apartment building, it is expected for there to be no pileup of bottles *at the house*—I admire this phrase of Billy's, covertly desiring its laid-back charm, its gritty stability of old and heavy cutlery, of ready soup stock in the fridge, but to use the phrase would be brandishing saddle folks' speech like it was mine.

My apartment is a dorm-style room with a small kitchen and a drip-dry bathroom you hose down. No tenacity or cleansers required. Just a squirt of Sexy Mild shampoo on a scouring pad and the tub-basin-toilet scintillate. My decor: a large-toothed purple comb, green tea body scent, and baby lotion in a country basket like at a Bragg Creek gift shop.

Nails trimmed. Copies of bank wires sent home. Passport checked every night. Socks darned (for my flannel pleasure). Panties even a bit fatigued, I trash.

"Ready for death?" is Billy's joke, the way I leave things shipshape. But his tax receipts and spare key are kept in my document drawer.

Away from home I am a light sleeper, timid even. A student's insight from class can jar me awake in the middle of the night.

"Teacher, young Koreans like fabricated food."

Seeing I did not understand, the student explained, "To fabricate means to lie, right? McDonald's burgers, instant noodles. Well, are they not cheating foods?"

He was darn right!

Often, trying to sleep, turning over and my feet making small half arcs on the fresh, cool side of the sheet, I hear him. The salary man. I call him the salary man because he walks in briefcase strides. The familiar tap-tap of feet behind rows of trees that separate the teachers' building from the street. Where does he go to in the wee hours? He coughs firmly but quickly, as if already in a packed subway and wanting to inflict minimum discomfort on fellow passengers.

When I give up on sleeping, often it is evening in Calgary. Calgary, where I do not drape my pants over the chair, where they lie bunched up on the floor. Cookie crumbs under my pillow. I call Mother: "Hi, what are you cooking?"

On a grainy envelope from Calgary, a postal code can warm my blood with thoughts of home; none of the la-di-dah of half-a-grapefruit nonsense, but thick winter porridge that sticks to your ribs. The comfort of home makes a dweller drowsy, like being in an overheated bus in the deep of winter. I may not want to get off.

However, for my language students, postal codes are rumpled tissues, forgotten at the bottom of their knapsacks. One day, I teach a class of young students to practice writing postcards, insistent on the postal codes.

"Teacher, the card will get there!" one of them groans, wondering if all English teachers are postal code pain-in-the-necks. I tell him that minus postal code his address will sag like a toothless granny's mouth. My vain lot all flash smiles, exposing pomegranate pink gums and ship-shape teeth. I change my technique. I tell them a story.

There was a lonely English teacher sitting on her yo on a Sunday evening, souping on instant ramen. Cars on the street were parked like sausage links because everyone was home and kitchen windows were fogged with steamy cooking. For the teacher, nothing was lonelier than Sunday evenings. Her delight was the reedy pleasure she got out of gazing at postal codes on envelopes she received from friends and family. Some countries called them zip codes, others, pins. How her heart raced! The agitation of a slight pounding at the temples, as if a headache was coming along, only it did not. Postal codes made her sit up. She was not lonely then, on a Sunday evening, caressing envelopes, far away from home.

A good story works. Melodrama works better. Without further protest, my students hunker down and highlight both the sender's and receiver's codes for my pleasure.

When I teach, my smile is past bright. It is loud like the ripping call of a moose for his beloved. I refuse to deliver ho hum instruction without Smucker's Jam pucker.

"Hi, my name is ____. What is your name?" (American contractions can go to hell!)

It unnerves my students that I do not use the grey English textbook, so that they might cram English into their suitcase brains and travel to their exams. Instead, I am their dreaded customs officer, who excavates material from newspapers, pats down a headline or a blurb, and frisks phrases into action.

In the *Korea Times,* when a famous climber refers to Everest as "the big hills," I relish the way he familiarizes those gynormous peaks.

I tell my students, "The climber's homely phrase for the exalted mountain is casual. Familiar."

"What is familiar?"

"It is like a kind neighbour leaving rhubarb from his garden against your back door."

"What is rhubarb?" a question from the back.

I try to answer their questions while demonstrating that "English is tasty as jam!"

I cringe against the thought of them all dropping out, hoofing it for the door.

Imagine the prairie teacher on her teacherage: a cameo brooch at her throat. Her hygienic hands. The young teacher makes sure there is not a trace of green fertility on her face.

In the small hours of the night, when I cannot sleep, I plan the prairie teacher's perfect hair. It is always swooped back (like in films) except for one irrepressible tendril that submits to being pinned back in the mornings, but during sluggish afternoons falls over the teacher's cheek. The young farmer mumbles that he fell in love with the teacher's kiss curl.

How did the prairie teacher endure desolation, alone at two in the morning, sleeping without family?

The prairie teacher kept things trim and tidy.

What if, on the off chance, the head of the department visited my place? What if I was ill and the university doctor had to make a house call? You would not find tired panties in my drawer. In Chonju, I have a penchant for order, like Calgarians' obsession for lacquered gardens when flowers intuitively want to spurt low to duck the ribby winds. (Was the prairie teacher really fastidious by nature?)

And the giving.

Did the prairie teacher ache from so much giving? I get parched, hard as a betel nut, dry as a lizard. The sweet of the mosquito coil in my throat, I watch my thickened hand swell out of the damage of giving to students, and answering my students' questions:

"You like Korean food?"

"You have boyfriend?"

("They are not grilling you, they want you to feel at home," a Korean friend of mine told me once.)

"Really, you eat rice for breakfast?"

"Really."

"Teacher, no sandwich?"

"No sandwich."

"Sandwich is cold."

"I know."

"Where do you eat?"

"Il-mi Mandu."

"The dumpling place?"

"Yes."

"You like Korean food?"

"Yes."

"You a taangol customer at Il-mi?"

"Yes, I am a regular."

"And the teahouse?"

"I am a regular at the teahouse as well."

Most Koreans like tearjerkers. Before any of us have TVs in the teachers' building, on the rooftop at 9 p.m. Texas Billy and I witness the same heart-wrenching serial flickering in the one hundred and twenty living rooms of the apartment complex we face.

"Cold fruit goes well with tears," is what Billy says. He cannot stand Korean soaps, and he cannot stand fruit. When his students bring him some, he leaves the bag hanging around my doorknob.

When at last we have TVs of our own, I want to watch *The Green Mile* and Billy comes over to watch it with me. He has seen it a couple of times. He tells me what is happening as I have my head under the quilt most of the time. When the film is over, he heads to 3 x 3; and no, I cannot join him. He needs a break from me.

One day in a taxi, the driver is suddenly irate. "American women cannot sacrifice like Korean women."

"I am not American."

"Where you from?"

"Chonju," I reply.

"No, no, where are you from? Indo? Indo?" he asks.

I look out the window, frowning at the sidewalks whizzing by. I have been in Chonju over two years and am worn to the bone by the scintillating chat. Sometimes my limbs are awkward, like a child in someone else's hallway who has pegged her coat on the hook and then finds herself at sea. I do not have to be a dry husk. I could be a tacky pleaser like a film star in a tabloid.

"Where are you from?" The taxi driver, desperate.

I give up. "Canada."

"But you're Indo!"

"I am Canadian."

"Are you shitting me?"

At 5:45 a.m., when I head to the store down the road from my apartment, snarly hair over my eyes, I do not want to prattle. I want to sleep. I want a carton of milk.

No pleasantries, only milk.

The shopkeeper puts four hugely expensive breasty apples in my bag. I scowl. He shrugs. I scowl harder.

"Just because," he says.

The turning point.

A crack in my hide.

"Why are you breaking my heart?"

But the shopkeeper does not understand. Or does he? Once, he pats my shoulder, like he does comprehend my tatterdemalion state, the distress of being away from home, when he says, "You look tired. You must miss your family."

Outside the hairdresser's next door, a discarded Styrofoam bowl of Ramyeon. Red pepper flecks on its sides, stained lipstick chopsticks neatly on top, as if the litter is already disposed. Someone's very early breakfast. The sun not even out, and two washed quilts hang over the balcony of the opposite apartment building. An ordinary day begun, and yet, not quite.

Something slides back into place; a boon, a tender boon from the shopkeeper.

A day given measure.

In Chonju, Texas Billy and I co-teach continuing education. His morning class has mostly homemakers, fifty-five-year-old women. During Billy's period, I hear his students shriek in the next room. Waah, it is husband, big boss, or surly mother-in-law the teacher is impersonating.

I teach a whole class of middle-aged government officials from various ministries, all male, required to take English for promotion. Men from a generation reared on hand-me-downs. Theirs was a childhood of hunger and sorrow. The rancour in their voices pervades the room.

"The red in my mother's cheeks faded faster than a ghost's apparition."

"She was rubble under a heartless mother-in-law."

"Mother salvaged pot, rag, even a curl of mushroom."

For them, a woman in the workplace is an office flower. I am a supplier of metaphors in their dotage: an endless hand, a bulky, shady tree, a dogged, cowardly immigrant who holds tight to her seat under a banyan tree. No need to be Tommy Douglas and fight to change things.

For many immigrants, Canada-time is assumed to be time to pay taxes and relax in a country where orange school buses are secure as bonds, homes unscathed, white patio chairs safe in the yellow yard light. Still—no point in getting the fuddy-duddies riled up. No need for me to walk into the classroom with aggressive breasts, slamming doors like female detectives on TV. I subvert my neck. Like Koreans say, "The ripest rice bends the lowest."

But the trick is, in the end, I get them to careen my way.

I rekindle stories dear to their hearts, stories of the hardworking mother whose floors are shiny last thing before she goes to bed. My voice soft as the beginning of a ballad, giving them time to remember their mothers, mothers whose backs were bent like a shrimp's from years of toil; giving them time to be pensive, when I bring in stories of brides, brides fragrant as sesame oil.

My voice thickens when I introduce them to a Korean poet for whom the word "feminist" also includes men who understand women. When I tell them that the poet is the age of their university-going daughters, they are surprised. They do not want their daughters, their weakness, to endure the hardship of their mothers or the cruelty of mothers-in-law. That the poet speaks with the voice of their daughters pricks their livers.

One evening I am ready to tell them a story in English with the bit of dirt that they have been wanting all along. Their grins, sheepish as my college students.'

"True story, Sonsaengnim?"

"Yes, about a woman on Indian Airlines. In the eighties, India was not the power economy it is now. Now, of course, things have changed, but still I wonder, how much has changed underneath? This woman was from a small town, a young woman on the plane with her son, but they could not get seats together. An older man with piles of English papers, whose polka-dotted, yellow silk cravat looked like it bore many black eyes, was seated next to her. He offered to change seats with her son. The young woman said her thanks with the curls of a green chili on her lips, and then instructed her boy to do the same. When she thanked him again, she slipped in a bit of Hindi to let him know that she was not a western woman who could smile at a man with ease. She had her modesty to think of. 'Thank you, Ji,' she told him. 'Ji' is a polite way of addressing another person, like here, we say Sonsaengnim, teacher, when we address others with respect."

"English is not prized in India?"

"Oh yes, but it has lines of demarcation of its own. For example, only the wealthy can afford to send their children to convent schools. Others learn scruffy English. Back then, India's booming economy had not stormed the country. Now, most have satellite TVs and cell phones, but back then, a mofussil town girl talking in English casually with a stranger could mean a woman was a swinger. This woman on the plane was not from the upper crust where men and women drank scotch together and spoke very, very proper English. The woman thought, 'What if the man takes a chance up in the sky, treats me like I am a backless-dress thing?'"

My students do not understand the story a hundred percent, but grasp its nuance.

"She wanted to protect her honour?" one of them asks.

"For her, English was too free."

"Or, how you say Sonsaengnim, I can say f____ in English, but not Korean. I would be mortified if my children heard me swear in Korean."

"Not true, Park Seoung-chul! You were swearing like a stable boy last night at the bar."

And the mood lightens.

These evenings, my fatigued lot of students expect me to please them. They want candy language, jiggly Jello language, and friendly winks from their female teacher from the prairies. Please, no riff-raff topics. No hyena in petticoats, please.

It would be satisfying to tell them, "You lot are tasteless as sauce-less rice."

Does the nicotine from the Omar Sharif cigarettes they puff on all day and the overflow of soju and beer in their bloodstreams shoot green poison into their cheeks? My greater fear is that my young soldier pupil from another class I teach, my class joker, will become one of them.

He has begun compulsory military service. He will not rejoin the university for two years.

"First time sleeping alone," he tells me at Il-mi, where I invite him for lunch. He means being away from his mother. "When I return to my barracks, I turn my body to the wall. You understand, I must cry without noise."

I wanted to put my palm over his at the restaurant. But my student is a draftee, already a man. He has filled out. His nape and knuckles are massive.

"You wrote in your journal that you had acne because hormones were making your body tall."

"Really?" he asks. He cannot believe he was a kid only a year back. Laughter had been easy then. "It used to be thrilling to go on overnight trips to the mountains with friends, not waking up in my own bed. For breakfast, Mother would not be able to plop bits of her fish into my bowl of rice."

I want to ask him if away from home he thinks of his mother's floors, squeaky clean last thing before she goes to bed. I too want to confess what it is like to miss home. But he is my charge. How can I? I have to extirpate harshness from his life, fill his massive bones with chants, redden his mouth with cherries. My pupil will not know that his teacher checks and rechecks the gas stove before going to bed; that on a Saturday night, she sits on her yo eating fruit yogurt with a plastic toy spoon the shop clerk throws in; that she worries who will toss aside cushions, crouch low for her mother's reading glasses when her brother is at work. Have you got your keys, Mother? Why can Mother not accept that at her age, her workout at the Y and a Co-op expedition are too much in one day?

I do not want my infectious student to become a boss-man, but the process has started. He knows how to use a rifle. He is protecting his country. He is not doing some Level 4 work either, under Public Service, wearing a green uniform and minding a subway station or shuffling papers in a sleepy government office. There are other rites into manhood he will soon endure; perhaps he already has, like soldiers in the barracks collecting money to send an uninitiated one to a brothel. Rites, protocol, guard duty, ready to stick their lives on hold for twenty-four months, no fuss. In time, my soldier student will become impatient with the reproach in women's eyes.

I have a friend in Chonju, a fellow teacher, and we like to speed down the road in her green Matiz. Come Sunday, we drive into the country. Twenty minutes outside Chonju and into blue barley fields. Korean mountains have the femininity of draping sleeves.

One day, in spring, we jab-talk like it is scrambling away—

"You have chong for me, the way you are peeling that orange," my friend says to me. From every piece of orange, I remove the whiny, white threads, offering her pieces of bald, sweet fruit. "Why are you doing this for me?" she asks.

"Just because," I tell her.

"That is chong! Just because."

"The shopkeeper down the street from my place gifted me apples out of season, just because. Is this chong love?" I ask.

"Not exactly chong *love*. Love is fifty-fifty. Chong is not half-and-half, and often unearned."

My friend always refers to her car, her house, as ours: "I am waiting in our car."

"I think chong is unrequited love," I tell her, "unrequited" a word Korean students use all the time vying for romance, and the other is "nostalgia," especially around autumn, when leaves burnish gold and maroon, lost lovers are mourned, and films are drippy with teary separations. In autumn, Koreans grow wistful, and the word "nostalgic" runs rampant in journals, bars, coffee shops, and the public baths. I never hear the word scamper across the table in Canada. Maybe "nostalgia" in a French film with subtitles at the Plaza Theatre. But usually the word grows dusty, on dusty top shelves.

"We Koreans think marriage salts better with chong. Love is a fixed price, sly tests, the rigidity of anniversaries, this deal for that. An older sister may have chong for her younger sister, but the younger one continues to live on, blank as a page."

Tanzania continued on without Grandfather. The daffy love he had for the country since he arrived when he was nine.

"Often, the ones smitten are asked to piss off," I tell her.

"It happens all the time," she says, clutching the wheel tighter and stepping on the gas.

In my class, one afternoon I write "chong" on the board.

"Chong means to love without incentives," a male student offers.

"You mean you are looking for a goody girlfriend?" a young woman's retort.

"Chong is skin. Only you wear it for somebody else," another contribution.

For me, it is a moment of recognition. Ping! Is not Ganesh, the Hindu elephant god's carrier, a mouse? Because of the chong he has for the elephant god, the mouse has no idea of the gynormous load on his back.

"Have you seen a picture or a statue of the Hindu elephant god?" I ask my class.

Most have.

"He is the remover of obstacles, the kindest of the gods. Do you know what he rides?"

"A Ferrari? But he is more than king-size." The joker. Laughter.

"Do you know that the elephant god's vehicle is a mouse?"

Naturally, the class is in stitches. I wait for the last titters to fade.

"Disobey your eyes. Do not look at the elephant's size like your eye shows it to you. Do not be its servant."

"Teacher, I see what I see!" The joker.

"Other deities ride swans and tigers, but the elephant god, who is the remover of obstacles, rides a mouse. But if you ask the mouse about the colossal weight on its back, it will say, 'No, no, no! The god only looks samurai hefty, but his ankles are curvy as a dancer's. I flip the fudge-sweet god left, and then flip him right on my raggedy, long tail. It is a funny thing we have between us!'"

The joker asks, "Why is the god wearing an elephant's head?"

"In a fit of rage, his father lopped off his son's head."

I have their attention.

"The elephant god's mother instructed him to stand guard outside her door while she bathed—he did not have an elephant's head at that time. The father came home from the forest and wanted to see his wife. The elephant god would not budge from the door, and in a fit of rage the father lopped off his son's head. When the mother saw what had happened, she ordered her husband to fit any living head on her son, pronto. There was a herd of elephants passing by."

"What happened to the poor elephant?"

"That I do not know."

"Teacher, what do you mean? What a terrible story!"

The mouse's chong for the gynormous god is lost on my class. The endearing hero for them is the elephant who lost his head. It was his day. Why not? Ganesh would not mind. But I glimpse my blue sunflower startle, the bump of travel, grasping at contradictions (a mouse cannot carry an elephant, but the carrier of Lord Ganesh is, indeed, a mouse), accepting the charisma of perception, the *ping* that, through stories, we are sausage-linked. Yes, a mouse can bear an elephant's weight. And nothing belongs to one tribe.

My friend and I on another Sunday drive: this time for scrumptious fish stew by a meandering river, in steamy August. The wind picks up. A cyclist's white shirt balloons at the back, splitting into two puffy baguettes down his spinal cord. I do not look forward to getting out of the blessedly cold car, only to be engulfed in stickiness unpleasant as lying on a plastic sheet to have my legs waxed. My glasses fog up.

"You are my woman in the clouds," says my friend, locking the car.

In the steamy pour, I feel spiky as a bird out of a bath. Such dulcet chong from a friend, just because. Not even seven baths could be more refreshing, simply heaven flip-flopping in my mouth.

In another season, one thing porous and soft about my friend is that she wears a red winter coat nipped at the waist. It has a dancer's flare. On a day when Chonju's snow spreads festively, "You do not get dumped on," I tell her. "In Calgary, I shovel the sidewalk twice over."

But I miss trudging in the mush, two feet deep, early morning to catch the bus, eyes burning, cheeks on fire, and the sky pink. The bulky, blue city bus coming around the corner on tortoise legs. Time to blow my nose dry, the watery snot will freeze in an instant. More stomping, so my feet will not freeze.

In Chonju, during the first snowfall of the season, lovers gather outside the Old Gate at Chonbuk National University, a spot to watch and be watched. On their promenade, lovers leave behind crunchy foot tracks.

"Look at them leaving a trail of booty hearts," my friend says.

She and I have no male company with whom to share the first snowfall, when stalls that sell gloves and flowers do a roaring business. Il-mi Mandu jam-packed, everyone in the mood for the restaurant's steamy dumplings. A tendril across a woman's mouth, her lover caressing it away, their snuggled-up walk and pillow talk enough to crush someone who has no one.

But that evening, my friend's boss rings her up and delivers the dagger straight: "You have no boyfriend to share the first snowfall with, so my husband and I will take you out."

Her boss shares the elders' and farmers' sentiment that plenty of rice has made young Koreans soft. Now they want fancy ribbons around flowers. When my friend says she is not in the mood, her boss tells her to pout is foolish beauty.

Chong unwashed as a farmer's speech can be a prickly bush nipple, especially when someone's red winter coat has a dancer's flare and one is surrounded by exotic snow.

I tell her, "Someone thought of you. Peachy or prickly, chong's gust is sweet."

No one asks me to share the first snowfall.

But have I not received a bounty of chong? Chong is not Christmas, plop in the lap. It comes sporadically, in small, startling bursts, and I receive it often—sometimes I do not even know it until later.

One holiday in Puri, where pilgrims visit temples and tourists hit the beaches, I received wildly undeserved chong.

I was at a café. A man behind me rustled his newspaper. When I finished my breakfast, I left. Days later when I returned (since I had become a regular), the owner told me as he set down my usual, a stake of crunchy toast and a pot of coffee, "You know, the Bengali babu, the pilgrim from Calcutta, was watching over you." At first, I did not remember the paper rustler. Then wonderment. On a beach occupied by backpackers, someone watched over me through a whole meal. I was not alone!

The day before in Puri, when it was not even twilight but a hard blue beach afternoon, a fair-haired woman with a creamy Lucerne complexion (it was easy to tell she had just arrived) had been reading in a corner when a drunk whimpered he wanted to sit next to her. The owner was in the kitchen. She could take care of herself, I thought. Perhaps when he grabbed her, it would be time to intervene. Other backpackers got busy as well, staring at bony cows outside the café and the bright tide. Her boyfriend came a few long minutes later. The drunk pushed off.

Why had I not instantly come to her rescue? What if she had rebuffed me? Travelling can bring out the strangest reactions and it gets lonely. Sometimes, I ache for a rub right between my shoulder blades.

I wish I had looked back at my protector from Calcutta. But when does one return their gaze to the bus, or the airplane, or the café one has left? There is a boat and a commuter. Like home, a boat stays anchored so others may bustle off to occupations, temples, marriages, wars, and adventures. In Calgary, I learned of a poet, an alley clanger, a butterfly, who might tell you to hush, not a word, watch the river instead:

You walk.

The river stays.

This snowy evening in Chonju, restaurants are full of ochre with the heat of candles and eye nuzzle. I am happy that my friend is in one of those restaurants sharing a meal with her boss and her husband. I make my own boot prints in the snow. Then, soft as a kiss, home grazes my nape, and I see in my mind's eye the two familiar patio chairs in our backyard that remain toppled all through winter. But I see them at the end of the season, when it is no longer winter, when the first crocuses jut out, and I sit the patio chairs upright and wipe them with a wet tea cloth, then put a lemon-coconut square in the oven. The season for company has arrived. Mixing bowl washed and the square cooling on the kitchen table, I nip across the bald, brown fields for a bunch of tulips from Safeway.

In the East, a teacher is a banyan tree, forever giving shade and knowledge.

In Chonju, I stitch up my femaleness. I wear pants and long skirts to the university. My silly weakness is to jazz up my hair. Other women have the softs for shoes or French pedicures. I do my hair in braids, ten to twelve, and pull them into a ponytail at the crown. The prickle of sudden, shortened braids about my neck is pleasing. Then, for two-three days, I will not bother with hair grooming. The other style I can do blindfolded sitting on the toilet is:

first I brush my hair a hundred times like heroines of the past (who had grosgrain ribbons in their wardrobe) then pile it up slip-slop, one loose pile on top of another, Goody hairpins balanced on my thigh, finally, a head shake to allow the hair to settle into shiny, dishevelled rolls.

My special hair treatment has always been a quick vegetable oil rub in my scalp before a wash. Essentials, that I bring with me everywhere, are brown elastics from the hair shop in the snazzy Banker's Hall on 7th Avenue in Calgary, Goody hairpins, and a wide-toothed purple comb that has been with me forever; no mirror. I have never mastered how to use a curling iron. And my hand tingles from the buzz of a blow dryer. Even when I cream butter and sugar for a sweet loaf, first I pad the mixer's handle with a tea towel to lessen the sensation.

"Teacher, this style is cool!"

My students also say, "Teacher, not to worry, it is blue Monday." Decoded, "Your hairstyle stinks." They avoid a direct "No." It makes them cringe to say anything negative. Not to a teacher, sacred as a banyan tree.

"Have you finished?"

No response.

"Did you like the story?"

No response.

"It was an assignment."

No response.

"You remembered the assignment, right?"

Pin drop silence. Heads bent.

"Teacher, *you* are bossy!"

"And you are slackers!"

Sheepish grins.

A teacher must be devoid of sexual appeal, but one who entertains is venerated. Her lusty oils are reserved for edification, her spittle for books. When my dress buttons came undone once, they were dismayed.

"I am not lizard-dry, you freaks!" I wanted to scream.

May 15th is Teachers' Day in Korea, when I get flowers wrapped in pond green wrappings and gifts of barrettes and sentimental cards.

But my real holiday awaits around the corner.

For all my vacations from teaching in Chonju, I shake off the invisible but gargantuan hand stuck to my normal arm: a scorpion cannot stop from stinging its rescuer just as my teacher's hand cannot stop from giving. But then, on vacations, my holidays, I go to meet my Beloved—

> for a tryst with him in Mogul Delhi. He, waiting at Indira Gandhi International, we will breakfast at the Imperial, we will sip dry martinis, I will listen to bawdy Hindi pop, and my shirt buttons will slip-slop all over, and he, my Beloved, can slide in his hand any time.

Boarding

At Gate B11, I am useless. The real Canadian has already proved up.

We stand to board, the line going nowhere. The Albertan hero up front.

"How do you say thank you in their language?" a woman, about seventy, asks the hero. Her husband beams, and so do the Alberta-bound, friendly folks in the queue.

The Albertan obliges, his face a tad sideways, bashful in the way of small town boys.

"The women in Japan are dolls, aren't they?" she asks.

The woman feels no compulsion to rinse her hair blue like women her age on city buses, prattling on with the driver. This woman's rough hair shags her face. Her cardigan conveys that she has been cocooned. It is long and expensively knit, with buttons of wood. One knows that she has always had her husband by her side to open doors, to listen to her back-seat instructions.

"You married to one?" No one shushes her. She has that kind of karma.

The Albertan's "yes" is without fanfare, plain as a husband's daily routine of placing a glass of water on his wife's night table.

There is heartache of a difference between the "yes" of a Canadian and that of an immigrant. An immigrant's "yes" is not steady. She is still finding her feet. I did not dig wells or erect fence posts. I carry the debt of unearned domicile in my "yes." In minus twenty degrees, when one nipple turns west and the other east, I am not one who has survived a log shanty with a sod roof. I find casual, backdoor prairie words like "sod" and "slough" snooty as stilettos.

We board the plane to Calgary.

The plane hums.

The book I have with me on the plane is from Billy, about cowboys' way of life in Texas, their recipes collected by a Texan rancher and chef. Billy ordered it for me from San Antonio. The photographs are magnificent. Chuck boxes have shelves and compartments to hold sugar, flour, and utensils. Three buttermilk chess pies cool on a rack. One chuck box has a beaten-up, black clock with numbers in gold, lending it a BBC steadfastness.

The Alberta hero found a wife in foreign Japan and sensibly negotiated the hurdles. Her family. His family. He married her. Everything fell in place. He would inherit his father's cottage by the lake. He could take on the new, a Japanese wife with vigor, delighting in the refreshingly different. When a venerated prairie poet as a child was warned by his Aunt Agnes to not swallow cherry stones or a cherry tree would grow out his belly, he shuddered at first. But then he was thrilled, for he had never seen a cherry tree in Alberta.

Cherry tree.

Cherry blossom tree.

How will a wife from Japan call the prairies her home?

My Dear Under-the-Rose,

Flying out to Canada, my new home, I did not know how to love a new land like I loved Cheka Cheka Creek in Dodoma, as well as Ramson's Cinema, and Koti Kamanga who wore purple socks and spelled dictionary words with an unsquashy calm. I did not want to love you for food, laundry, and good money. But I told Maa to forget Persian designs for my pillowcases.

And then I met my Beloved, not in Canada, and, first, in a dream.

My Beloved, a carpet man, has two rugs woven for me with crocuses, spits, harvest moons, and elephants decked in Saskatoon berries, tender-foot getup, not Persian motifs of hunting scenes and stylized floral.

Loving my Beloved, as I love you, is also an act of imagination. I do not want to wake up one day, the flour around my belly eternal, as I roll out another chapatti, that will melt in his mouth, with harsh, quick fingers. I could not bear if he ate up my years like this. Verity for others is in the cornflakes-vinegar stability of home, but not me.

It was not a dream in which I first saw my Beloved. It was a nightmare. I saw a man with a hooked nose, unshaven. I haunted him in his sleep as well. I was wearing a blue sundress, the same one that I wore when we finally met, in Old Delhi. Was the nightmare a premonition that our relationship would be catastrophic? So far, it has not turned true, still our dream is a frightening puzzle. We were panicked, so scared, that we kept dodging each other for many weeks. Things changed. Now, for twenty-five years he has been leaving jasmines under my pillowcase, buying me bangles in Agra (where we timorously held hands the first time), and buttering my morning toast.

Despite my arousal for anticipation, the unexpected, there are two kinds of rushes that do not ride easy in me: Mother's breath (I continue to creep into her bedroom to check on her breathing). And, the kind of sudden rush that comes when you realize you have become used to something: my Beloved, counting a wad of bank notes, or buttering my morning toast.

When we part for another three-four months, it is hard. I am bent as a serf, smelling everything: his ashtray, his bathroom slippers. His empty cup of tea I leave alone for a week. I shun his pillowcases altogether. They would do me in.

You, my under-the-rose, are my blue bin sky. And my Beloved, he is the pheromone trail that somehow always leads me back to you. It could be his prairie-dry pucker of a kiss. Either way, I wait for you both, on edge, when I walk out the sliding airport doors, hoping you will be there, waiting for me.

> Girth and a quickstep,
> girth and a quickstep,
> left my earring, search for my earring,
> on the prairies, the prairies.

Speak Gor Gor Sweet

Even in June in Calgary there are still electric plugs dangling in front of some cars, half in, half out. Two city buses, one behind the other, waiting for the lights to change to green, take up almost the entire road. I like to watch drivers tip sideways as they turn a corner. The CTrain coming all the way to Crowfoot now, I may not have to buy a car after all, if I ever return for good. Crowfoot is expanding. At one time, there was nothing much beyond 53rd Street, a few exclusive shops. I bought a set of wine goblets from one of them. Now nouveau Crowfoot with its spread of circular plazas confuses the heck out of shoppers unfamiliar with the area. ("Is the shop that sells black candles in this plaza or the one across the street?") Against the backdrop of the purple Rockies, shops have green-framed windows and pointy roofs, Calgary-Swiss Alps decor. Calgarians now want black candles. What would the legendary Mrs. Caroline Fulham think of Calgary gone la-di-dah?

Well over a hundred years ago, the Queen of Garbage Row kept pigs in her backyard in downtown Calgary. They feasted on garbage from downtown hotels that she took home in wooden barrels in her wagon. Mrs. Fulham was also very grubby. One day, she went to see a doctor, one of her legs was bothering her. Upon inspection, the doctor bet five dollars, pronouncing that in the whole of Calgary there was not a leg filthier than the one she was showing him. Mrs. Fulham's head must have swayed like an elephant's, trunk thrown back in celebration (I imagine her scarf crusty as a scab) as she triumphantly unrolled the stocking off her other leg to prove him wrong by producing the filthiest leg in town. The doctor paid up. It was not a good idea to goad Mrs. Fulham.

And today, 7th Avenue's glitterati and those who drive the smart CTrains would be leery of her, watching out for the garbage queen's wagon to lurch from around the corner (she had her own rules). If she were alive, she would be with the boys at the Alberta Hotel, knocking back a couple of afternoon beers.

One June afternoon, I stop at Brewsters for a pint of Flying Frog. Then, while the florist is wrapping my purchase of bearded purple flowers, I pop next door to the Dutch bakery for a loaf of nutty sunflower bread and liqueur chocolates for my brother. That is when I see the HSBC bank across the street. Its spiffy logo reminds me of a white bow tie against red. I step in.

When I spotted an HSBC branch on Barakhamba Road in New Delhi, I was thrilled. If need be, money could be wired from the Crowfoot HSBC, a fifteen-minute walk from our house in Calgary, shorter in summer if you cut through the fields.

I greet the front desk clerk like we are both wearing maple leaf pins. You have seen the greeters at Calgary International wearing cowboy hats and red vests, smiling at the incoming passengers? They are NICE! They are the kind of neighbourly people you could talk to over the fence. I have not seen them at airports in Vancouver or Toronto. I smile at the clerk as comfortably as the greeters. Right off she asks if I am Canadian. My smile grows cold. *Peaches, you are still fresh off the boat.*

The clerk sticks to her guns. "The question is right on the form." Her shoulders have teeth.

"I am only making inquires."

"But are you a Canadian citizen?"

I nod.

"Then please fill out the form."

Her "please"s and "thank you"s to immigrants must be ample as sesame seeds. And the twang!

I stare at Ms. Shania from HSBC. Ms. Shania stares back. Only when flustered, an immigrant's accent stumbles. With me, her accent does not unhinge. She is in charge. I am a sample of the riff-raff mosaic that has walked through her glass doors.

I walk out; however, not before I get personal. "I guess you kow-tow to real Canadians, the gentle giants in flannel."

Stupid cow. I cut through the fields. She is the kind of immigrant who would have the country's fare of blueberry muffins down pat. Her home decor must be muted. Too bad her exotic flannel-wallahs have already moved from pastel to the warmth of ochre and teal.

This is one kind of immigrant. There is another. She is the kind that shortchanges fellow immigrants on privacy, dismissing it as white folks' ailment.

Another summer day, in the lingerie section at The Bay, a sales-woman is hell bent on doing her dharma. She asks me with a spoon-against-the-pot clarity, "What kind of support?" I have not sought her fine fettered advice. Everyone around is welcome to listen in. Then Madam strides into my fitting room, bossy as a married sister who knows it all. "Try this one," she instructs, thrusting a bra in my face. She does not smell of rosy sachets like real lingerie ladies. She smells of no-nonsense cloves.

Of course, immigrants like to strut: the Ferrari in the garage, a mansion in Mount Royal, accents of course, private schools, nan-nies, and piano lessons. They also have a demented mall rat side, not for food, but scampering to carry out toothsome deeds for fellow immigrants, like the saleswoman giving me ghetto-to-ghetto life breath. I was breathing fine on my own.

In the end I do purchase the bra she chooses. Actually two, for she does have a perspicacious eye for a superb fit-o-fit. But why did she signal me apart, right away my older married sister, when I wanted to wear my hat at a rakish angle? Sometimes, the space eked out by one immigrant for another is narrow as a coffin.

When Harrison Ford eats straight out of a pan, his sexy attributes swell, but a middle-aged immigrant at his beef curry, his nipples crunched by the table's edge, is a sorry sight. Willy-nilly, he thrusts his hand into a Wonder Bread plastic bag, tearing bits of white bread with his fingers. The last thing he cares about is a tureen or a butter plate. He is still looking for a job, or keeps a stiff upper lip being a parking lot attendant. Meanwhile, his wife, who is out earning, wants red roses and dexterity in bed (I am not sure of Madam who smells of cloves). He will not try anything new, not even the fit step towards brown bread. Plunked in front of his 24″ Sony TV, he closes off. His wife has shed off pounds and joined the new country. In fact, she pullulates towards its opportunities. The new country fixes up women saucy and autonomous, like Madam, like Mother, who until she retired a couple of years ago, walked about downtown during her lunch hour in her sturdy walking shoes, her hair not coloured, no-nonsense chin-length, but glossy from salon treatments.

"Have a nice day," Madam wishes me earnestly. On leaving, I overhear her telling another customer where most of the Indian gold shops are located in the city. "Best price for twenty-four karat gold jewellery," she reports.

The customer thanks Madam profusely—one does this when one thinks an immigrant is an eager beaver, especially from places that she has not heard of like Bagamoyo, or Sancha, as if they need more humanity than settlers from Europe. I wish both would stuff their goodness.

When I was younger, working and going to university, I hankered to be part of the Canadian shindig, eager for black second-hand corduroys (another way of wearing a hat at a rakish angle). Back then, I was a good secretary, devoted as a daughter-in-law. In office practice terms, I executed my duties of coffeemaker-cum-detective-cum-wife with lethal efficiency. In Dar es Salaam, I garnered secretarial skills and worked in a distant relative's grocery store as well. I wanted to be useful in Canada right away.

So when my boss, a Calgary professor, did not recognize a name on the pink message slip I left on his desk, I helpfully added, "The caller, she had an accent."

"Don't we all?" he retorted with a wink, liberal Trudeauist that he was in our hick town, proving me a "wannabe." I should not have mish-mashed immigrants into a big pot of rice and moong beans. In his snazzy yellow bow tie, the professor emerged as the enlightened one, a jihadi of pluralistic Canada, setting me straight on accents. Past his head, the prairie sky whooped blue with laughter. I shrank. Against the professor's twinkling retort and his blue bin sky, I showed up murky and unlit.

Accents aside, there are things in the country I would rather leave alone—Lazy Susans for one, those revolving discs in the darkness of cupboards, stupidest things to clean. And snow, remote as blue blood. I comply with the city's rules to shovel the sidewalk after a snowfall, even sweeping away the icing sugar kind. It is best to keep out of the way of the icy queen who splinters the hips of gingerly treading immigrants.

When I am in Chonju, on Sundays, already a lonely affair, I take a Tylenol habitually like afternoon tea and buy an almond Häagen-Dazs bar to savour the cold that reminds me of home. These Sundays, there is no waiting at the checkout counter, no cartful of groceries to unload, then shovel snow and bake a couple of sweet loaves, the final weekend chore. I have all of Sunday's forlorn leisure to myself. Usually I ring my Beloved in Delhi.

"Are you eating well?" he asks, his verity. He is already bothersome.

Why then do I not seek out Grandmother's commodious small talk? Or, there is always my brother, ready with a droll comment—but at times small talk and droll comments rattle me the way handy but cumbersome Lazy Susans do.

In Chonju, when Monday's lesson is planned, work shoes polished, the apartment smelling of cold, clean sheets, I climb upon a bus to while away the hours until suppertime.

Rotted-shoe pickled cabbage stinks up these buses. Under their seats, farm women put away pots of kimchi wrapped in sturdy scarves, three knots at the top. In Dodoma, as Grandmother used to say, the middle knot Shiva's third eye, splendid and protective. I smile at the women as if they are calling my name. I have seen many a mother climb the steep, uneven steps to her daughter's hostel to bring her homemade kimchi, or cross the street for a taxi, anxious to rush to her married son's house with a warm pot. For her, getting kimchi to her child is like waking up at two in the morning all over again to feed her little one. She is in the same state of dishevelment and urgency, riding a bus, bundle of stinky love and garlic galore in her thick fingers.

That is verity.

I travel because others remain moored.

First thing home, my bags stuffed with gifts and still in the hallway, I bake. I have missed ovens. Cherry squares done, my Beloved calls. Hearing him, my hair feels longer, indulged. The scent of rhubarb and cinnamon apple clinging to my hair.

"What are you wearing?" I ask him.

We in the family are not privy to Maa's courier arrangement with the Sonara from Dodoma. And it suits us not to ask when a Mr. Patel or Mrs. Modi, strangers from Gujarat, ring the doorbell asking for Grandmother. We know heirlooms are returning to her. Meanwhile, we have walked on. Overcoats and twenty-four karat jewellery in the same step are much too much to lug. Maa's gold stays in the bank, her precaution if a war breaks out: what if Muslims are ordered to leave Canada? Go home?

But where is home?

Over one long weekend, when Grandmother was first time gardener, we had her backyard dug, rowed, planted, and labelled before dark. We worked with the demonic zeal of the ten-headed Ravan of Lanka. With iceberg lettuce, we staggered the planting of seedlings that Grandmother had started indoors, keeping the soil moist.

"I will plant the rest every three days. Then we will have a nice spread, no?"

I asked, "How long before we can eat the lettuce?"

"Oh, ninety-five days or so."

But when the lettuce was ready, we were not prepared for its effeminate green.

"Blonde lettuce," Grandmother called the fair, quill-light leaves. The recipe we tried was an orange poppy seed dressing. We never made it again, unnerved by its sweet exude.

"I have a coconut for a brain. My gardening book says that the inner yellow leaves are sweet, but we added more sweet to already sweet."

Grandmother's gardening book has drawings of herbs and herby words like catmint and Roman chamomile. They make me want to join a quilting class. My favourite drawing is a trough bursting with horseradish, a black and white rooster in front. When Maa first started gardening, she liked to tap out an ink pellet for her fountain pen as if it was a cigarette and then, into her gardening journal, copy the information she fancied: to pickle beets quickly, put them in salt water with a piece of rye bread. It sours them within a couple of days, another tip from the Ukrainian Cultural Heritage Village (even though Grandmother had no interest in pickling the root vegetable, only lured by its red tint).

"Brown-eyed Susan," I rolled off slowly.

"Names of flowers must be Persian beauties. This brown-eyed Susan sounds like a girl next door."

"In Dodoma, you would have thought a flashy name was hullabaloo from the rooftop."

"Not anymore!"

"Whooee, spring!"

"This year too spring will take her sweet time," she said.

"Maa, when my friend, who sleeps with her window half open even in the middle of February, was a little girl, she sucked honey from the stems of buffalo beans. Not even poisonous. Like in our backyard in Dodoma, behind the mango and jamun trees, where wild flowers leaked milk too, you remember? Sticky milk that made your fingers swell."

"Tell me, is not 'buffalo bean' a shameless name for a flower, like a stud in heat?"

I tried to be funny with Maa about the failed lettuce. "Sweet on top of sweet vegetables, we are developing Canadian taste."

"Hah! And all immigrants eat food so hot, it makes their eyebrows water."

"You sound like Grandfather!" For him the word "all" was like brandishing a sword in the air.

"Right to the end, it was his way. The rest could go to hell."

When would she forgive Grandfather?

But I had no need to be morose, no issues.

In Goa, "no issues" is the local, cool expression. It means "no problem." Goa, Goa.

When my Beloved and I meet for a tryst in Goa, it is constant foreplay: gym, sauna, watching kingfishers by the ponds at 8 a.m., breakfast feasts of omelettes, sausages, jaggery pancakes, maple syrup, dossas, upma, porridge, parathas, rice pudding, papaya, pomegranates already seeded (like we are royals) in a cut-glass bowl, waddling for a gin and tonic (to cut the grease) at the breezy patio bar, again kingfishers by the ponds 4 p.m., a languid swim, another beer, and nipping into town for freshly caught fish.

For long days in Chonju before Chuseok, when for the harvest festival baskets of food are laden for family and friends, and the teachers go for endless beef-barbequed dinners, I sip only kirsch and black currant sorbet. My hair spilt down the side of my face, I greet Texas Billy at 3 x 3 with a smile irritating as a housefly.

"You are already with your boyfriend," Billy complains.

In response, I recite Mirza Ghalib, a famous Urdu poet during British rule in India. "At last it is here / I receive recompense / For the anguish I endured so long."

"At last *what* is here?"

"Love, at last love is here."

"You're hot and ready, but your flight to Delhi does not leave until tomorrow."

"Billy, Billy, don't say Delhi, say *Dilhi*, all in the mouth like a French kiss."

"Yeah, and I gotta take a leak."

Neither my Beloved nor I belong to a flag, pedigree, crest, or identity. It is just him and me. Two utterly selfish backs, one curved inside the belly of the other, evicting the rest of the world.

Only with Allah I toe the line, laugh with caution. I do not show Him my reckless teeth. In this, I am sensible like my grandmother.

Or, I do as I please but quietly, like Mother. No hyena laughter fanfare.

In a Punjabi love story, ancient as the hills, Heer chooses her beloved, Ranjha, over God. Crazy Heer does not play her cards right. God Almighty is in the palm of her hand, she can ask from Him anything, but all Heer sees is Ranjha, and Ranjha, and Ranjha.

Like Heer, I am ribby for my Beloved. For him, I would dance on a white sheet strewn with glass chips oblivious to pain, yet my taut body would be alert. Through storeys of mattresses, I would be able to feel the bump of a pea digging my back. But unlike Heer, I am not fearless.

When Heer cannot find Ranjha, she lets out such an ear-splitting scream that God Almighty is rattled. From His throne in the sky, He descends to earth to cajole her to leave with Him. Heer could have waffled with cunning. God does not come down just for anyone. She could have gone to heaven with Allah, and pleaded in the place of abode for her Ranjha. Instead, Heer says to the Almighty, "But You are not my Ranjha." That is a kind of hyena laughter in God's face.

In love, Heer is asinine. In love, Heer is more sincere. She would not settle for anyone else, even God, only Ranjha, Ranjha, Ranjha.

Allah, Allah, Allah.

During our first hymen days together, my Beloved and I are painfully shy of each other.

At Incheon Airport, I wait for him for over ten hours. Visiting me in Chonju, his plane from Delhi is delayed due the capital's infamous winter fog. The kind coachwoman at Incheon, whose services finish at 10 p.m., waits with me past midnight. When my Beloved and I sit coldly beside each other in her shuttle bus, she says, "Get close! Get close! You have not seen each other for so long!" We are mortified.

One time when he meets me at Delhi's Indira Ghandi International Airport, he hobbles across the meeting area because his new shoes pinch his toes. We stop by a seedy stall to buy him a pair of rubber slippers.

The light bulb, in the stall where we purchase his slippers, is so dim my eyeballs jaundice. On three plastic plates are piles of condoms with pictures of women with over-ballooned breasts; they stand a bit tilted as if the circus weight on their chests would otherwise tip them over. The shopkeeper also sells massage oil, pink tissues, sliced white bread, batteries, and Bisleri mineral water. My Beloved buys rubber slippers and three bottles of Bisleri. When I ask him for money, he pulls notes from his wallet with the bashfulness of a honeymooner. I purchase a bottle of green massage oil. It reeks of joss sticks.

I am wearing peach silk lingerie underneath my clothes; that morning, it was still wrapped in tissue from the Cat's Pyjamas in Calgary (something from home). Outside, I am clad in well-worn black pants and a white shirt (an old nuzzly). On the flight to him, I could not manage a tizzy wait as well as animated colours. Dilhi, Dilhi, Dilhi. It is a French kiss.

There is a mangy, white dog outside the teal blue stall.
    A cow walks by.

One afternoon, my Beloved and I go to the South Extension Market in South Delhi to buy fresh chicken. Fresh alive. I notice the hairs around the sides of my Beloved's ears. They are delicate, but long, and actually quite dark. And the weak quake of chickens. Huddled in their cages, a very few eat grains; most of them in jerky sleep, their half-closed eyes pus yellow. We will return in twenty minutes. (Even fresh meat diehards do not want to see their meal killed in front of their eyes.) Butchers in movies are rotund, always standing. At Safeway, they have CEO haircuts. This one sits at his job. He is scrawny and holds a knife between his toes to slither off fat. A tiny old woman, extremely well scrubbed, with diamonds in her drooping earlobes, tells the butcher with the flourish of a dowager from Old Delhi, "Sir, you know, purchasing the choicest stewing lamb is one of my few pleasures in life."

The butcher gives her a corner smile, romantic as Elvis. The flirtations beneath transactions during winter afternoons in Delhi are savoury as arched eyebrows. When a qawwali of boisterous and competitive claps plays on his radio, the butcher turns up the volume.

When we return to the butcher at South Ex., there are no telltale feathers on the slippery stone floors. But the criss-crossing drains gurgle like waterfalls in a Chinese restaurant.

Drunk on this shandy Delhi afternoon, we strip off our own clothes easily, though still shy to remove each other's (the season will ripen). He sprinkles water on the floor and turns on the fan. The fragrance of baked earth fills the room. I open my legs to the fan. He had not brought me flowers at the airport; this time, he brought me purple grapes from a farm two hours away from the city. First he went to the barber, then to Khan Market to buy himself a pair of pants and a shirt like it were Eid, and then headed to the farm for Sonaka grapes. Sonaka sounds electronic. Those were his preludes.

He takes a grape and tests it on his skin as if milk, and feeds me, one by one.

"Too many," I protest. "Chicken, now grapes."

Soothing my belly, he tells me, "There is something for you in the kitchen."

I put on my T-shirt. This modesty too will dissolve in its own season. On the table is a garland of jasmines to girth my hips. He comes behind me.

"When did you manage this?" I ask.

"When I miss you, I plan things."

Right in the kitchen, he parts my legs, not as gently this time. The familiar smell of pencil in his sweat. We are afternoon lovers.

Dear Allah, play favouritism. Temper with my season. Ripen it slow. And I will not let you down like Heer.

When things between us become commonplace, I resent packing his things in my knapsack: his eyeglass case, a scribbled phone number, or his cardigan.

"I will not be cold," he says.

"And then you are."

"I am from Kashmir. I am used to the cold."

"And I am from Calgary."

"Where even the garage is heated."

With clenched teeth obligation, I still stuff his cardigan in my pack. It is easy to be a cowboy when you have a nester ready with your goodies in her bag.

When he offers to carry my knapsack, I am disdainful. "I do not want to carry your things, but I also do not want you to carry mine."

"Why you are spoiling for a fight?"

"I am not!" I protest, frustrated that he does not understand. Running after him like a mother with his sweater. I detest it when he wants a bite from my dish. Way to go conk out passion.

Where Grandfather was dessert, my Beloved is a savoury. English, as well, is dessert: service with a smile, twangy, and so bright you need shades. It is also a language fixed in mathematics.

- "No Madam, you tell me how many apples you want."
- "I want the shutters down."
- "Let us take turns with the armrest."
- "Here is what I owe, $3.24."

A transaction in English works on absolute clarity. Stark yellow mustard on bread. Purchasing a pair of shoes in Calgary a long time ago, I asked the shoe clerk, a round-faced teenager with a Band-Aid forehead, to throw in a couple of tins of shoe polish stacked behind her. The old-fashioned art of indulging a patron, some fragrant tea or a hot towel press before a leg is waxed, was not part of commercial decorum.

"You mean you don't want me to charge you for the polish?" She was bewildered.

I stared at her. How could I have been so horrifyingly misunderstood?

The clerk was equally upset. "You weren't clear!" she said.

That was a long time ago, when salon leg waxing was a novelty, and I took a long bus ride from the northwest to the northeast part of the city to a woman's house to get the chore done. But still, selling in Canada lacks dance. Our house in Dodoma was not the kind where things were ever plain.

"Even when you have had enough pudding and the second last bite is unpleasant as a brolly's poke in the calf, that is okay, because the next hankering for sweets is around the corner. That is how a house reigns in a dweller, numbing rebellion with sweets. What do I always tell your grandfather?" This is what Grandmother always asked me in Dodoma, training me to be restrained as her subtle Swiss watch.

"To speak gor gor sweet."

"That is right. Sugars are trappings. A home likes it this way. From the start, she harnesses dwellers with the taste of sweets because of their rudimentary nature: sugar at the top, sugar in the middle, sugar at the bottom. No surprises. What is a bride's first morsel?"

"A sweet."

"A baby's announcement?"

"A sweet."

"Breaking a fast?"

"With dates."

For all its sugar might, a home's transience is palpable. Any time, it may fall to pieces. I have an urge to remove my shoes when I see a luggage lock no bigger than a small, square, metal taviz to ward off evil, or a beauty shop in a small town that promises a desperate range: Beauty Parlour-cum-Nursing Home.

Or when a three-year-old is still mumbling prayers when rescuers pull her out from under the rubble, fifty-two hours after an earthquake.

Such gestures make me weep as if I am on high blood pressure pills. The hymn sung at dawn at the jamatkhana chafing my heart again:

> Rise awake my shallow soul.
> Why are you wasting your time in slumber?

I want to go home. The familiar protects and nourishes.

"I miss Grandmother," I often tell my Beloved.

"It is 5 a.m. in Calgary. You want to phone so early?"

"What did you have for lunch?" Grandmother might ask. She is seven seas away, the line is brilliantly clear. And the permanence of her question anchors me.

"Please bring the banana sweet," my Beloved said to me one time, "alive." He meant he wanted it unpeeled.

Grandmother avoided making her explanations overly clear. She said people bit into your shoulder otherwise. Grandfather did just that, being plain, most times offensive in his clarity, and upsetting most people in town. When bitten, he was oblivious or did not care. Not Grandmother. Her face, like the black leather watch strap she wore, was a sliding door, precise and hidden from view. In Dodoma, Grandmother had the sensibility of savouries. She peeled and added layers according to the storm she had to weather, and food arrived at the table on lavish platters: mounds of chapattis, rice, eggplant, beef and chicken stews, never the dainty moderation of two tiny samosas with a wedge of lemon on a gold-rimmed side plate. Ours were busy with windmills, bonanza-loud, like Grandfather's explanations. My Beloved never piles his plate at buffets, no sudden famine gnawing at his heels, neither does he wave his fork for punctuation. I watch his plate, done, clean as a whistle, his upper lip swollen as a pregnant woman's.

Would Grandfather and my Beloved have gotten along? Grandfather had a raffish charm; my Beloved is persistent, even when there is no room to dance.

At the Old Delhi railway station, my Beloved drives a tough bargain for a taxi to take us to Shimla one day. The manager of taxis acts pliable. He is not.

My Beloved begins a new dance, "You are like my younger brother, you know."

The manager is pleased, though knows perfectly well the butter has been laid on thick. His chubby body burgeons theatrically, chest to hand, he says, "Older brother, now *you* have got to listen to me."

He is going to rip us.

"Typical immigrant thinking," I hear my brother's voice. He and I would shake our heads in amazement when an uncle or aunty from Tanzania would take their sniffing stand. In Canada, they were either hard-done-by or they would hold up their forever-and-a-day generic racist card, limp with overuse.

Well, I do not trust that manager an inch! But me a racist? Though I confess, I would rather be on the 24th floor of a five-star, swanky bar, sipping a dry martini, away from the grimy trees, whose trunks, though solid, make me think of bony chickens. I want respite from the persistent smog, dusty-brown, like the rind of comté cheese. Delhi's winter sun is sinking, and there is a sudden explosion of mynahs in the sky as they head to their nests.

I return to the manager's cot of an office, where a courtship has begun: charismatic, tricky, savoury, and full of bargains. One of them will leave with the heavier pockets. This time, it is the manager, whose laughter is gallant as a host's, bidding us adieu, "Go in peace, brother mine." But the taxi he sends us the next day is squeaky clean and the driver a native of Shimla, who takes us "rounding" for the best deals in town, hotels, meals, and excursions. When we leave Shimla, our pockets are still nicely full.

"That was a fair exchange, no?" My Beloved, pleased as punch.

"Did you predict this would happen, that in the end, we would save money anyway?" I ask.

"Not initially, but when he told me, in winter, he likes to put hot water bottles in the beds of his guests at home, I knew we would get excellent service, so I stopped negotiating."

"When was that?"

"When you were outside watching the birds."

When I am in Chonju, my Beloved's postcards trail across my kitchen, or I leave a letter from him propped against a kettle of sunflowers, or the envelope and pages scattered across the quilt, my bare thighs. His slanted writing brazen, still in bed. In Calgary, his letters arrive in white envelopes, postal code squarely ironed.

When I am alone, but in a festive mood, I treat my feet to a good scrub and paint my toenails coral. "Madonna colour," once suggested a cosmetic-wallah, brandishing bottles of steel red nail polish. He had not observed carefully. Realizing his miscalculation, that I was no Madonna-walli, my notebooks giving him the lead, he says, "It's Tabu's favourite, maybe yours too?" Tabu is an actress who also writes poetry.

Petroleum jelly aside, I carry a tub of foot scrub and a terracotta pumice stone, two staples in my backpack—which I pretend is a sack, the kind adventurers hurled over their shoulder on the train heading out west to the prairies for free land the government promised. I want the hurly-burly of a pioneer's spirit to rub favourably on my Eddie Bauer backpack. "Sack," I whisper, in awe of the adventurous pioneer of the 19th century, riding the Canadian Pacific out to Alberta, whereas I am a spoiled immigrant who has never lived in a log shanty. My prairie contribution is romance and insubordination, like cocky Trudeau throwing bottles back at the crowd. Gawky admiration for Trudeau, for sure. The cowboy boots and ascot he wore to work certainly got the goat of his more conservatively dressed peers, but only made Grandmother and I weaker at the knees.

The grainy foot scour smells like the liquorice Black Cat bubble gum of my childhood. It reminds me how Grandmother poked gum into the potato duck with the back of her eyebrow pencil for its eyes, our first afternoon in Dodoma. I continue to scrape my heels in short, hard scrubs. I wonder what happened to the Tall Woman I stood behind at the jamatkhana in Dodoma? Most of the Indians settled in North America or the United Kingdom. She disappeared with her family to Europe. Even after she joined Grandfather's party of dissenters, bringing black market Chivas to the meetings in the Dead Office, she continued to unnerve Grandmother, who kept out of her way. She wore minis when the government stipulated maxis. Police officers wielding kibokos in their hands ignored her. The Tall Woman had Ganga power.

At the guesthouse where I am staying, there are no soap bars left by travellers on the window sill, the slight space travellers share.

Though we almost never meet at the guesthouse itself, we are privy to one another's soaps: Nag Champa, Mysore Sandal, Medimix, even cucumber soap from Korea.

A final scrub, a good rinse. My feet scintillate like temple cymbals.

Boots laced up, one last check of the drawers before I vacate the place.

When I want to gossip with my Beloved, girl-to-girl kind, to remember our markers, he denies them.

"Of course we kissed," he means the first day we confessed at the Taj Mahal in Agra. My Beloved is adamant. We did not. A martyr's fierceness rises in me. I will not correct him!

There is a growing impatience in his voice. The easygoing privacy he lent me in the early years forgotten, or, he does not want to remember.

"Why do you talk like we are always young, soft in the head?"

My Beloved, still a munificent lover, now prefers a domestic flame. His middle-age girth, gutting fresh fish, and one day, when he butters my morning toast, it is routine. I left that kind of home at seven. I want an affair. He has settled into the daily.

One trip, when I receive bangles from him, a ritual in our courtship, he does not slip them slowly on my wrists.

"Let's zip to the Taj. Then head to Akbar's for kebabs. What do you say?" he asks, not once glancing at my wrists that I have attended to, overrun with glass coloured bangles. It is like the chore is done and he has ticked it off his shopping list.

I inhale the familiar smog of Agra. My dress is the colour of dried persimmons. A button has popped off. He asks, "When will you mend that?" He has asked me twice now. One time, my disarray would have made him smile. Still, my body floats above errands and rules. Suppers being cooked, children bent over homework, wives handing leftovers to the watchmen ready for night duty. I sip my holiday of bangles, savouring the sharp bites of soft hairs mowed down.

At night, my Beloved is less parsimonious. I know before midnight he will buy strands of coral jasmines for my wrists or tuck them under my pillow. He insists it is a Mogul custom. I adore his outright fib. For now, I am content to look out the car window. I spot a magpie with its upturned long tail and whisper to it to fly to the Korean peninsula, fly to Deokjin Park behind the university and pluck a voluptuous lotus from the pond. Let it keep my gargantuan hand company. They say a teacher's hand cradles a student and that a lotus cradles the world. Then I shake off the plea. I do not want to think of anyone else and steal another look at my Beloved, a candy glance away.

One evening, my Beloved kisses my shoulder and leaves the car to buy Kashmiri kebabs and handkerchief rotis at Nizamuddin in Old Delhi. One would think the rotis would resemble a handkerchief's diminutive measurements, but they are about 14″ in breadth, thin as parchment.

I savour his kiss. His lips not wet pink like a love god's. His pucker, prairie-dry, grazes my shoulder.

The shrine of the 14th century Sufi saint, Nizamuddin Chishti, is just behind us.

He parked the car away from the scuffle of the street, close to a park, but still privy to a dusty, buzzing Delhi winter night. Green banners of the Prophet decorate shops, some with silver tassels. A loudspeaker blasts a fighty mullah's taped speech. Has he swigged the crazy, over-salted waters of Qum, the city of imam-schooling in Iran? His sermon is noisy as wedding crackers.

I sip my cherry holiday. My Beloved's kiss, a dry burn on my shoulder. I count three foreign money exchange stalls, four S.T.D./ I.S.D. (Subscriber Trunk Dialling and International Subscriber Dialling) phone booths. Men saunter hand-in-hand. Women move swiftly, the pavement not theirs, tugging children and bundles of laundry.

Saint Nizamuddin must have whirled in Allah's arms, submitting unto Him his floppy weight. Is my worship a slur? Should I wrap my bones tight like the scurrying women? Allah from Arabia is ways-a-way in China. My Allah throws me fierce red tulips.

People squeeze in and out of the tight parking spots. The best kebabs and tandoori chicken in the whole of Delhi are grilled on this street, a hop and skip away from the Saint's shrine. I imagined Nizamuddin beefy as Grandfather, his skin, getting only indoor sunshine, with an ivory hue of Moguls illustrated in miniature paintings. Small boys employed by restaurants swish plates under the street's taps. My Beloved relishes the fact that here he can buy a five-star hotel meal just shy of a hundred rupees.

I watch the business of others. My Beloved awaits our kebabs.

Moments slip past.

A short distance off, there is a bicycle rickshaw man with his back hunched as he counts his day's earnings. During the day, I have casually glanced at these riders' elongated backs as they wait for passengers to hitch up into the perched box. Seeing a rider now, so close to me, I feel myself grow embarrassed. Passengers usually haggle them down.

Goats in the park are busy searching for greenery at night.

A Kashmiri youth always makes our kebabs, his neck fragile but his chest sturdy as a plank. Did his mother lay down her headscarf at his feet, begging him not to go across the border to Pakistan to become a freedom fighter? Did she send him on a bus to Delhi instead? Perhaps she had seen him playing cricket with the freedom fighters, or had he asked her for money to buy the Kamachi shoes the freedom fighters wore? They were the cool dudes, haute stylists, who wore bullets for precious stones in their rings. Let others fight for a free Kashmir, not her son.

First time I visited my Beloved in Srinagar in the late 1980s, I saw the city of houseboats and wooden bridges through a shattered car window. Someone had a thrown a stone at his car as my Beloved was speeding to the airport to pick me up. Of the seven bridges originally there, only two survive. They have a new bridge with a doomed name: Zero Bridge.

My Beloved, like others, left Kashmir so that he may live. I have always known him as restless, unable to settle, yet with every departure away from Srinagar, he hankers to return, even for an unhappy, unsafe couple of days—that generally escalates into months—of terror and curfew. When a bandh, a Hindi word meaning "closed," is lifted for a couple of hours, Kashmiris scurry to buy vegetables and staples, rush home, barricade the doors, and wait and wait and wait. For thirty years now. When my Beloved tells me of his mother feeding him roasted eggs in winter, or him dancing on tabletops at college, it seems like exotic and happy cinema. At bedtime, he often sings to me. One is a wedding song of an anxious groom standing under a cherry tree, his aunts singing to him, easing his fears about the big day. Now, at weddings, songs sung are about injustice and pillage.

"My Kashmir is dying and no one is helping us," he tells me.

He disappears inside the restaurant. Sometimes he stands on the steps to wave in the direction of the car. I wave back without rolling down the window. Anyway, he cannot see me, and I do not want to wave and set beggars mewling, like insistent cats around the car until I relent with money.

The door clicks open. My Beloved drops a bagful of hot kebabs on my lap. Thin and lavishly large handkerchief rotis wrapped in newspapers tied with thread.

"Okay?" his tender checkup.

I breathe in smoky placations of food, curling spiky and savoury. And the expiration of moments. Somewhere in Kashmir an Indian soldier is frisking a Kashmiri, elsewhere in the valley, a sullen baker is closing shop. My tears would bewilder him, so I ask him the practical.

Did he get the coriander-mint chutney? The tiny pink onions marinated in vinegar? What about green chilies?

"Sing to me about the unsure groom under the cherry tree."

"Now?"

"Now!"

He sings it twice because it is a short song.

We pass by my favourite Mogul tomb with yellow cat's eyes. On very grimy nights, the bulbous dome is the bluish-yellow of congealed bruises.

"I just saw a pronghorn from the Rockies in the Mogul emperor's gardens," I tell him. A fib, of course. But I wanted the blue prairies there and then, Mother's two gold bangles clinking as she heats soup or unlocks the front door.

I long for my prairies. And I long for him, who is right next to me.

The hymn sung at the jamatkhana, seizing my heart:

Rise awake, my shallow soul.

Why are you wasting your time in slumber?

With both my lovers nudging me to Allah, my soul is not shallow, but perspicacious. Is this how Grandfather felt in his outpouring for Allah?

"You saw the mountain goats from Banff?" my Beloved asks, skeptical, the expression on his face doubtful as a child's.

"The emperor's barber is buried in those gardens."

"Really?"

The gardens used to be beautiful. Four hundred years ago, the emperor's Persian wife had his tomb surrounded by a Persian garden. Now rubbish litters the gardens. Pots and the ragged laundry of squatters are drying on the dusty shrubs. The living in full swing, in the garden tomb.

My professor friend and I drive around Delhi in her snappy car for whisky. I wish I had bought a bottle of Jameson back at the duty-free shop and saved us the workout. It is no mean feat to drive on Delhi's jammed, ill-lit, air-polluted thoroughfares with male drivers ready to ambush. They wait for the "lady driver" to fug up, make a bubbly swerve. Then they blast horns with the mirth of a clanging wedding procession. Thoroughfares are their turf, making brisk economic turns their god-given endowment.

"Brother, we have to buy some whisky for our guest. Which is the nearest place you know?" we ask the attendant at a petrol station.

Here in Delhi, even middle-aged women waffle when they ask for whisky.

At the liquor shop, a swarm of rickshaw-wallahs, truckers, office peons, and servants bob towards the window. The attendant at the petrol pump did not say the nearest liquor shop would *not* be our best bet. Too many, you know, Eve-teasers, he could have explained. Maybe the detail slipped from him. He did not look mean.

Sweat surrounds me. I am the only woman in the mob. I press my left hand to my bum, palm outward. What if someone sidles up my backside?

My friend is still trying to find a spot among bulky lorries. We drove to the liquor store with lolly thoughts that it would be in a well-lit plaza like Khan Market. There would be a pharmacy, a shoe shop, an herbal soap boutique, a bookstore playing new age music, and a bustling twenty-two karat gold shop with guards sporting saloon-trimmed moustaches. I even imagined white patio chairs outside.

The men shove to get to the window and stare at me as well, not daring to come close. I am like Mama Zu-zu terrorizing the town of Dodoma. These men fear me. There are waves of twenty, fifty, and hundred rupee notes above their heads. I wave a five hundred rupee note. Some rest their hands on a pair of shoulders in front, and if the man is short, then they rest them on his winter headgear, no offence meant or taken. I am riding on their shock. If it becomes replaced by a look of the tiger-playing-with-the-kill in their eyes, I will hurtle forward, faster than a prairie wind. I hear, "Ladies first. Ladies first." Two Sikhs in South Delhi's double-stitched outdoor sharps divide the motley crowd with authority and a have-a-heart kind of charm: the Red Sea parts for me to walk right up to the window.

"Thank you."

One of the spiffy Sikhs replies, "But lady, it is our dharma."

At the counter, I expect a harassed worker on matchstick legs, but it is the owner himself. He has a startling black moustache on a face creamy as an Indian sweet.

I will never again turn up my nose at the word "lady": lady doctor, or ladies first.

Alone in the crowd at the liquor store I cannot help but remember the time when, on a busy highway on the outskirts of Delhi with my Beloved, our taxi's battery died. The driver was scrawny. People helped push the car, and suddenly one of them grabbed my Beloved's shoulders while his friend reached into his back pocket. My Beloved did not miss a beat, his Kashmiri war wits about him. He shrugged off the man's grip and went straight into the light, in the middle of the highway, amidst cars, bicycles, scooters, buses and trucks, screaming, "He is trying to steal my wallet!" The two thieves melted into the dark.

The car started.

One unforgettable day, I headed from the airport to Lune Guest House in Old Delhi, where I knew the owners. I had cut my stay short in Srinagar because of a recurring nightmare. They had invited me to their house, and told me their Kashmiri friend had just landed in Srinagar the evening before. He wanted to come to Delhi right away, just like me. They invited me for chai and stuffed parathas, after I had freshened up, and told me that he too would be joining us. Apparently, they had told him about me.

I put on my blue sundress, inappropriate for Old Delhi, but the rest of my clothes were in their washer.

When we first met, my Beloved stared at me. Though he was clean-shaven, I knew I had seen him before, in my dream. The hooked nose had not changed. He left after a quick cup of tea. I was relieved. My family was safe and I had recognized the man in my nightmare. Now, he would not bother me.

After meeting him, we were not right away together. I was not staying at Luna, and had planned my walkabout alone, this time away from medieval Delhi and closer to New Delhi of coffee shops and galleries, and eventually to see my friend, the literature professor.

An asshole followed me. At first, he hollered from his shop, Reliable Emporium,

"Miss, Miss, where you from? Come, I tell your palms!" and squeezed his palms against the sides of his chest as if they were breasts.

The guffaws. I could have stepped inside his stall and bought something to shut him up. But I did not. Once, little girls offered me flowers on a steep hill on the outskirts of Kathmandu, and then terrorized me for payment, breathing down my wrists. The two men also on the tour stood apart. After I had paid the girls wads of notes, one of the men said, "You're intimidated easily." No way was I going into the jerk's shop.

He followed me, making farting noises. He stepped up on the grunts and got himself a matinee show. Men in doorways scratched their balls with lazy relish. Others got off their bikes to watch. I made a blind turn and fled into a good-looking shop and met an indulgent shopkeeper. After dickering over the price of a statue of one-tusked Ganesh with a daughterly comeliness, lending the shopkeeper time to size me up, I pushed my purchase into my knapsack. Naturally, the shopkeeper charged me triple, but was charmed by my disposition. Now was the moment to strike.

"Sir, is there a clothes-washer near here?"

Immediately, the shopkeeper's hospitality jetted into flight. His young boy accompanied me to the laundry district behind the highway. Armed with an introduction from a respectable local businessman, soon I would be in a grounded place. He dismissed me gruffly when he told his boy, "Tell the clothes-washer not to charge the girl a rupee more or he will have me to reckon with."

I was ready to be looked after, and savoured the gracious shopkeeper's balmy endearment, *girl, girl, girl*.

In Tukuyu, after Mother washed my hair, I would wear my favourite red, polka dotted sundress. At the store, Father would admire my frock and I picked out my favourite Bensons toffees from the glass jar. Pockets full of Bensons toffee, swinging my arms, I joined my friends. My parents' princess.

The boy walked in front of me. For a short time, I would not be a furtive cat under a car trying to get away from a pack of street dogs. A woman's walkabout around Delhi is chancy.

The asshole hollered again. Dismayed, I realized I was back on his turf.

"Want it? Alone, Miss *must* want it, no? Free Miss, so tasty long *sheesh* kebab!"

The boy turtled his courteous head inside his shirt. His shoulders jiggled with laughter. But the asshole had lost his captive audience. They recognized who the boy worked for. Most withdrew into their shops. Soon I would be inside a grounded place.

In Dodoma, the Sonara regaled Grandmother with stories of the golden pair in the *Ramayana*, Rama and Sita. Sita had the fierce loyalty of Hanuman-the-monkey, the greatest devotee of Rama.

When Sita was abducted by the evil Ravana of Lanka, Hanuman set the kingdom of Lanka on fire, his saucy tail whooping up razzmatazz fires. He lifted Sita in his arms and returned her to her husband, Rama.

I have no loyal Hanuman to lift me to his muscular underbelly. And in some places where I travel to without a father, husband, or a son, the goombahs declare me without lineage. An unaccompanied woman is up for grabs.

So I set out to find my own stabilizers to map en route. My turfs are places that sprout fangs when the goombahs come meddling. In these protective sarais, I am inside a magical circle. Then I do not walk on short planks of legs. I am splashy as a cabbie dashing a salute to another cabbie zooming past.

One of the places has to be a clothes-washer's, who lends my clothes crisp mornings and a sense of work. Then my travel has measure. And a post office from where I send home postcards with lipstick kisses, sometimes sillies in cloth envelopes stitched by the tailor right outside, and sometimes, I post home wobbly hurts as well, like after the asshole followed me, making smacking noises with his lips and palms. No one came to my rescue. I wanted to be home then, doing familiar chores like checking on the bran muffins swelling in the oven. Instead, I wrote home. A mistake.

A deluge of letters followed: from Grandmother. Mother as well. They wanted me to come home. I phoned. Everyone wanted to talk to me, cousins, aunts, and uncles included. Why were they all at Grandmother's? Who cooked? Relatives are not guests exactly. Guests are treated to diverse dishes from Gujarat to East Africa. It is hours and hours of peeling, mincing, whipping and splattering, and finally, three garbage bags ready to be taken outside. Stubborn as the dark hairs on the chin, Grandmother's edict is clear: a meal with variety, from Bombay pompfret to cassava cooked in coconut. If disobeyed, she is ready for chest pains and the emergency room.

"Who cooked?" I asked.

They all laughed me off, for I have protested enough times, why not kebabs, mint chutney, and freshly made cherry almonds for the guests? Okay, mangoes (the most expensive kind) from Superstore. Instead, their conversation with me was on eggshells. They were patient as missionaries.

"You do not understand! That happened weeks back, I am fine now!" I wailed, irked further. I was coming off unoriginal as a teenager.

One day I fired a note to Mother:

> Mother,
>
> I was just eight. Why did you compel me to give the penniless girl one of my two new nighties? I liked them both. I liked the pink one *and* the yellow one, both from *my* grandmother. Why did I have to give anyone anything? I was not grown up. You said because she had not seen her mother in a year. I lost my father! I gave the stupid cow the pink nightie because I wanted you to stop crying all day, you, who told me to cry short in Tukuyu. Remember?

I headed to my magical circle: my place of meals where I ate without lewd comments from the truckers. The chai there was a mean brew Indian truckers called "the brawny hundred-kilometre kick." Here, the Cook-Owner of the dhaba, my protector.

There are dhabas where I have eaten furtively, where men suck on their cigarettes, balled fists against their lips. Smoke tatters edgily out their nostrils. They are biding time before the pounce: she is asking for it, this queer, unaccompanied woman. They know what foreign women want. All whores. In late night commercials, like the condom commercial, I have seen what they see. A Caribbean and an oily blonde, both with sweet, honest smiles, each gyrating their hips as if a man is already inside them. Then the camera zooms in on a dark male cooling the blonde's throat with ice cubes. The ice has the opposite effect. The female explodes into a Bond girl. She flings her leg around his torso. With a clean crunch she could strangle her cooler's ribs, she is so horny.

But these goombahs could never close in on me in the dhaba of my protector. For the Cook, I was his goddess Lakshmi of Fortune, putting down money for two square meals a day.

The sound of Mother's two gold bangles in my ears.

When Mother became a widow, I, her daughter, stayed at her side. In the first few years after Father's death, my strength poured into Mother's upkeep. But I have also harmed her, like with the occasional accusation delivered sometimes, when I am away, on a postcard. I know I will be forgiven, and this hurts even more. I call for her from my very depth: Mother.

"Today, the goddess is not in a first class mood, what is the matter?" the Cook asked.

The tears would not stop. I had finally piqued the truckers' interest.

The Cook folded his arms on top of his hurly-burly belly and yelled over, "What brothers, along with Delhi's power cuts is there also a shortage of women outside that you come to my dhaba to eat the heads of my customers?"

The truckers hastily looked away.

"Memsahib, cup-chino." The Cook brought me frothy coffee in a glass and two fingers of a Kit Kat on a saucer. "I shooed off those uglier-than-film-villains."

"I know," I said. "I miss home."

"If you were my daughter, I would not let you travel alone so far. Next time, come with your husband."

Instantly, I thought of the Kashmiri man I had met recently.

"Are you my Maa-Lakshmi?" I asked the Cook.

The Cook's eyes became round golgappas. "Miss, you have malaria? Head temperature is okay?" Here he was, treating me as a form of the Goddess, and I had turned the tables.

The Cook, good and kind to me, was my closest connection to Mother. I desperately wanted to hold the hem of his oversized, grubby singlet.

"When my mother cannot sleep, I pour hot milk over her cereal, slice in bananas, and take it to her bedroom, upstairs."

"Miss, maybe it is home time?"

"Maybe."

It was the clothes-washer who put me in touch with the Cook. It is often this way: one protector funnelling me to another, a system stable as a passport. Inside magic circles is how I travel on a chancy Indian highway.

How did the man with the hooked nose, who terrorized me in my dreams, whom I kept dodging in person, become my Beloved? Delhi is spread over 1483 square kilometres and has a population of 14 million, but I kept bumping into him at coffee houses in Connaught Place, on Janpath, at Humayun's tomb with its bulbous dome the colour of bruises. We were cordial, and very, very brief. I would sit up textbook straight, and flick him off with chaste, cruel eyes. It was instinctive. Then I left the city to travel to Ajmer to visit the shrine of Khwaja Moinuddin Chisti.

The place was busy but not as crowded as I had anticipated, and I took my time under a sprawling tree. And I began to think of him. A dull scratching in my heart that I could not get to. No one could. At the hotel, I huddled on the couch, telephone in my lap. I should go home. In Delhi, I would do some shopping, visit Agra, and leave India.

I went to a coffee shop behind the Indian Oil building. And he was there, the next day, haggard and unshaven, more like the terrorizer in my dreams.

He said, "I had already seen you in my dreams before I met you. And you were wearing a blue dress."

He sat sideways as if about to leave. The air around our table was tense, sniffy as armpits. We ate vegetable cutlets, but mostly we kept quiet. I confessed nothing.

I was going to take a bus to see the Taj Mahal the next day, but he was there at the Inter State Bus Terminal as well. He did not know why, but he wanted to go to Agra.

So that is how it started.

First he bought me glass bangles, and then before I stepped off the horse cart outside the gates of the Taj Mahal, my Beloved whispered in my ear, "Say whatever comes to your heart before you step down to see Mumtaz's Taj." The Taj Mahal appeared more reticent than graceful, I said, "Yes." None of the ribcage explosions followed. We held hands out of the courtesy of declaration. One day later, he flew back to Kashmir, and I flew home and walked in the icy field of an elementary school, thoroughly spooked.

That is how our long romance began, twenty-five years ago.

One day, in the bustling market in Lucknow, hours by bus from Delhi, where my Beloved is at a carpet conference for two days, I buy bangles for myself because of a song streaming out of a butcher's radio. A song from Mother's era, one she sang to my brother and me at bedtime in Tukuyu:

> To Lucknow, now do let's go
> My amiable, enchanting Rani.
> Let us leave Bombay's rotted waters
> My amiable, enchanting Rani.

Mother had four nights of moonlight. In Tukuyu, she wore red high-heeled shoes. After Father's death, she wore sturdy sandals, and later, boots in Canada. She had a lot of ground to cover.

I want festive bangles, now!

Grave as a doctor, the bangle seller applies pressure to the podgy part of my hand and then switches technique. His fingers croon, cajoling my knuckles. The bangles slide through like butter. The bangle seller's heat scorches my wrist.

What is my Beloved wearing today, far away in Delhi?

When we are together, he butters my morning toast.

We write each other harsh, lovely letters.

But at airports, we shuffle, shy, as if on a first-time date.

My glass bangles clink, gone Chinook, like joggers in balmy, twelve degree February.

Since our first time there, my Beloved never takes me to the Taj Mahal in barren, unbridal wrists. The last time he bought me bangles from an old man with a hennaed beard around the corner from the Taj, I watched from the car. Sitting on his spotless, white-sheeted throne with bangles hanging about him in grape bunches, the old man exhibited no whoop to sell. My Beloved bargained with runty pleasure. Then he ran down the steps, booty in hand. In the car, he jammed the bangles down my wrist.

"What happened?" I asked.

"The baba asked if it was my intention to wipe him clean."

In his untucked holiday blue shirt, his girl in the car, he bargained mulishly until the old man chided him and got him red in the neck.

When we are apart, I miss him so much. There is a crunch in my nose, like I am about to fall. I breathe slowly. What is my Beloved wearing today? A pirouette of bangles on my wrist, all I can do is caress them, waiting for a bus, finding a seat among strangers.

Arriving

On the plane to Calgary, an old man is mixing his coffee. Cagily he turns his cup this way and that. There is not much room on an airplane tray. After a sly shift he leans back to watch the effect. The flight attendant indulges him with packets of cream and sugar. He tears open four packets of sugar in a row. About to sip his coffee, he changes his mind. Carefully he sets his cup down. He knows on the plane he should not blunder on excess cream. He does anyway. His coffee must be sugar wax. He takes a tentative sip, gags, and jerks straight up in fright. But he will not give up. His shaking fingers poke about the squeezed food tray. There is much time on an airplane. Though we will be landing soon.

I smile at the old man. He cocks his head then checks his ankles. He moves them up and down as if warming up for a race. I smile again.

I remember Mother said when the nurse placed me in her arms first time, she did not know how to love me as a mother. She fell in love with me as if I were her newly born sister.

I check my watch. Soon, I will be home.

My Dear Under-the-Rose,

My Prairies, if I ask you, "What is a combine?" you may whoop with laughter. Then I will get huffy and call you a beer-chugging prick full of big ass auction numbers! So, I better not.

Instead, my under-the-rose, I will tell Grandmother to weave crocuses, spits, and purple sage on my first night pillowcases. Who embroiders these days in the age of crisp computers? But it sounds lovely, does it not? Like brushing your hair a hundred times before going to bed. If I marry, I fear my jaunts with you would stop and a vinegar-and-cornflakes reality would take over. I am like a renter who relishes the privilege of walking away from loss and cross-eyed grief. On TV, a ruined homeowner stands on one leg like a pilgrim, wringing and wringing his hands. His home flotsam, he begs God to set everything right, right as rain. He misses the irony. He lost his home in a flood.

There are elephants on the prairies in a tender-foot getup. Do your ears prick up? Girth and a quickstep, girth and a quickstep, left my earring, search for my earring, on the prairies, the prairies.

If you happen upon a pair of earrings left on the prairies by a broken-hearted lover, would you sob and sob for her? Would you come for her, all ribby hair, or slicing the air like a boomerang, hollering at God? Would you strike a wild deal with Him, do anything to get her back?

I say sunflowers, you say spits. I say barn dance, you say barn up.

May I decorate your lunch box? This way, lay a soft claim on you at the barn dance? From a lonely spot in a corridor, I watch your never-locked-hospitality of "Come on over!" You, my under-the-rose, so back-pocket-casual courteous. You, with your grand blue bin sky and your cattle brands. My love, when will I be branded flannel? When will you tip my chin, ask me to dance?

Will you send me heavy Goody hairpins? (I am always losing them.) Will you send spits, in an envelope, to wherever the heck I am?

I show you off in Delhi, a city of French kisses. Delhi does not know I have not smelled the wood of hockey sticks, but I tell them stories of a lover, cocky as Trudeau, his purple liver pulsing for me—this is you, my Prairies, and Delhi is moony for you, and asks, "When will that bola strutter come to fetch you?" Come to Delhi with red coals in your eyes for your blue garter claim. Come for the sake of others. They are watching me in Delhi. Come for the sake of decorum.

Do you even witness my re-departures? Do not call them exits. Even when on my journeys, I have trysts with you while I am in faraway places. You see, one who re-departs never loves casually. She never wakes up things only on a Saturday night. When will you make a U-turn like the cowboy at Ramson's Cinema? No, I will not lift my eyes to you. Why should I? Inside, I pull you to my liver. Outside I rock on them cool heels like, you sure are wasting my time. I even copy the lean of sullen cowboys in front of the general stores from a black and white Stampede postcard.

I am waiting, decked in swollen earrings, right in front of your eyes, both beggar and insubordinate aristocrat.

I am here today, gone tomorrow. Will you send me a love note back?

*   *   *

Trudeau died. Cancer.

I could have written and endured his withering eyebrow flick of dismissal (please Allah, please Allah, please Allah). I could have written when he lost his young son. Bloody immigrant coward, I was. Grandfather would have sent him a punchy get well, damn the consequences.

My Pierre, fitting-good to immigrants. Pierre, my Canada. Now, he will never know.

On my sojourn in Lucknow, when my Beloved is busy at his carpet conference in Delhi, a guide bows with a flourish. "Please allow me to be of supplementary service." Once the city was renowned for exquisite poetry, known also as a place facilitated by courtesans. I get weak the knees in the presence of a true Lucknowi.

Writers camped at renowned courtesans' doors to observe how they proffered scented paan to their varied clientele of nawabs, merchants, miffed poets, and idealistic students in riff-raff coats. The Lucknowi guide whisks me away for the tastiest kebabs, stubby oblongs that dissolve like butter in my mouth, on the very street where the famous courtesan, Umrao Jaan, resided some two hundred and fifty years ago. The guide tops off the evening by offering me a silver-covered paan, glittery as Eid, but he gives it with a hush, like we are sharing a cigarette after a very good night together. When he extends his hand, palm upward, I glimpse the underside of his wrist, where the skin has not tanned. This night, everything in Lucknow has the sensuality of butter and undercurrents. Not a peep of, how can I help him land in Canada of pasture-green tits?

It happens three weeks later. I am back home. The guide has mailed me reams of paper: a law diploma, various English courses through the British Council, a statistics course, computer graphics, and a spanking new fishing license. His postscript mentions he will also work as a cook.

Grandmother does not waste time on birthday cuties of socks with lipstick kisses. All her grandchildren get gold on their birthdays. Another form of currency lying in long, narrow coffins at the bank. When the clerk closes the door softly, I imagine a cortège of clerks with bowed heads outside, and take the shortest time to pick out the necklace or bracelet to wear at a wedding or another grand occasion. The clerk's ultra civility like I am a baroness (though the room is spartan, with a small table and two chairs, right at the back) is as discomfiting as a chef moving around tables, expecting me to be articulate about his flowers of the sea or schmancy cheese, "bocconcini."

Grandmother scorns Birks' eighteen karat displays. "Knick-knacks," she calls them, and dismisses anything short of a sober twenty-two karat nugget.

Only two sonaras have had intimate measurements of the women in our family: one was the Dodoma Sonara, and now, the young Pineridge Sonara, in southeast Calgary.

"Running from one sonara to another, I do not like that," Grandmother says. "One does not purchase gold like a deal on Arm & Hammer toothpaste, six in a pack. Jewels are sacrosanct. You wear them for adornment, but you also wear jewels to go within, to awaken and rekindle your spirit."

"Remember the hairpin he made for Jena Bai. She was so self-assured after that."

"She also became pitiless."

Not intending to dampen our afternoon, I ask about the Dodoma Sonara.

"He died."

"When?"

"Six months ago. All the gold that was he was keeping is now in the bank here."

"Lying in coffins."

"You ribbing me, girl? Come time to flee, dire need for gold is on par with oxygen."

"Was he ill?"

"Old age."

"Maa, he was your age and you are not old!"

"I am old but strong as a horse."

I curve my arm across her stomach. All is okay. Maa is with me, in her house in Marlborough, my mother and my brother are probably watching TV, at home.

"Now, the Dodoma Sonara, he was a pulse finder, readying the wearer for the journey inside."

"The women in Dodoma knew that?"

"Every one of them."

Home is where kebabs are served with coriander chutney, pillows plunked on top of the sofa for a slouchy nap, a sticky teaspoon in the sink and maraschino cherries in the fridge. But dwellers are not scot-free. I watch Mother's belly rising and falling in sleep. Anything ordinary is ultimately lavish. It can be taken away.

Tell me that I will see my Beloved soon, and my being is hued rosy red.

"Sahib is coming," a doorman may announce, the loveliest hymn reaching my ear. (I already heard his car in the driveway of the guesthouse.) He buys me Indian sweets in cities where we rendezvous, a vermilion-orange square, a pistachio green one, two with edible silver, in no-nonsense boxes. They remind me of the clean and hardy beauty of Shaker furniture. His languid, leisurely footsteps arriving, and my tinged, hurried heart.

Like Mother's breath, my Beloved does not ride easy in me. Anything, any time, may be taken away.

The doorman's "Sahib's coming," my four days of moonlight, the counting begun.

"You only have to open baby Krishna's mouth for a blast of Calgary sunshine," Grandmother says, as if she is back with her Sonara friend on a sleepy Dodoma afternoon.

The old Sonara was a devotee of Bala Krishna, the child god whose favourite pastime was stealing butter from houses of maidens. When they complained to his mother, she was always mortified. One day, feeling particularly virtuous like they had swept all the rooms, the embroidery and sewing done, the garments folded and put away in a chest, the maidens insisted that Krishna open his mouth. The naughty baby god shook his frothy head of black curls, but when Krishna's mother demanded he open his mouth, he obeyed, and she saw three worlds moving simultaneously inside her child's mouth.

"There was an explosion of Calgary sunshine in the god's mouth!"

"Maa, again you are embellishing!"

But I want to tell Maa that what sustains a traveller is the ordinary: bones for soup, cutlery in the drawer, blue bus tickets on top of the fridge, and the familiar barking of a dog.

On Sundays in Chonju, when my friend with the green Matiz cannot make it for our country drive, I go for walks and watch windowpanes in the neighbourhood steam up with mean cooking. This is the only day drivers park with courtesy for others, even leaving their phone numbers on the windshield. Mothers opening the foggy windows to call the children in and the smell of fish stew streams out.

"Cho Nam-il!"

"Kim Se-rim!"

"Cho Han-shin!"

"Park He-young!"

And I eat a cold sweet potato, or sauté garlic in a little oil to mop off with cold bread from the refrigerator, sleeping off the hours until Monday morning.

"Maa, ask the Pineridge Sonara to set my earrings in gold and silver, good omen metals. I want earrings with Plains Indians' dog tooth motif, good omen symbol. Let me show you, a chain of triangles, dog teeth, on the side of an earring."

Our Pineridge Sonara works out of a small shop sharp with fluorescent lights. His chunky ornaments are cooled on the top with sly filigree. Though he knows my neck and ankle measurements, finger and wrist as well, he never lifts his eyes to my face. The joss sticks gag sweet like Mohammed Rafiq, always crooning in the background:

> You are comely
>
> Dare I love you?

The lyrics make me giggle. The Pineridge Sonara likes the same songs heroes sang when they serenaded the heroines at Ramson's Cinema. The Pineridge Sonara flushes. His pompadour is sleek black and his breath smells of cardamom. What is most endearing about the new Sonara is that he wraps jewels in fuchsia paper, the size of a quartered handkerchief.

Am I imposing loneliness on myself? Waiting for a dog to bark when I cannot sleep, waiting for that brief heartening?

"Koreans say that if you are lost in the forest, listen for a barking dog, then a home is not far off," I tell Grandmother.

Maa phones the Pineridge Sonara and explains the motif in her words. She tells him, "When she is on the move, she needs all the good luck she can carry."

Maa tells me, "He says he wants to see a picture."

"I am leaving tomorrow!"

"Get a printout then. I will post you the earrings."

Goodbye Delhi.

My Beloved and I always stop at the Radisson, a few kilometres from Indira Gandhi, for a last martini. The final ritual. The olive in my drink, and I know my leaving is imminent. My Beloved's toothpaste packed in my toilet bag, to use in the airplane loo. Numb. Brushing my teeth.

And then I am home.

Where the key turns twice.

Where Mother's two gold bangles tinkle as she hangs up her coat. (She must have stepped out again and returned.) Where I snuggle deeper under the covers. (I must shovel snow first thing tomorrow morning when I start my brother's car.) Where I whisper in Delhi's or Chonju's direction, "Goodnight. Sleep tight."

Grandmother drinks the prairies like holy water, but at times, the malice done to her in Dodoma erupts with the cruelty of psoriasis.

"Satan's inferno came down on me that day when Jena Bai, whom your grandfather called his sister, had the nerve to tell me that my widowed daughter was not that badly off. How could she! My daughter was widowed barely a few days. She said to me, 'Think of girls widowed at sixteen. I know of a widow whose mother-in-law told her to go sit at the market entrance and show her face to men to earn her keep! Your daughter already has roots. She has children who will take care of her when she is old, and your husband is a powerful man.' And she called herself your grandfather's sister!"

Jena Bai and Jimmy-Jinxed surprised everyone by marrying and moving to Canada. When they arrived, Jimmy-Jinxed got a janitor's job at Footi Hospital, his first and only job in Calgary. To him and Jena Bai, it was never Foothills Hospital, just Footi. Even their ESL teacher gave up and called it Footi. Jimmy-Jinxed passed on, and Jena Bai now spends many weekends at our place, and on occasions at Grandmother's. She is invited to all family gatherings. But Grandmother is not her ally, not in Canada.

"Did you tell Grandfather?"

"He treated her like his sister. That was his business. I bore Jena Bai like I bear her now at my dinner table sloshed on her medicinal gin. You saw blisters in my mouth, child, but there were blisters in my liver as well. It never fails to surprise me that liver slices so easy."

When will Grandmother forgive Jena Bai?

Mother very early on had a dream in Calgary that our house in Tukuyu did not have a staircase. Then she understood. Tanzania was over for her. Now, her visits back to the country are touristy. She buys beaded knickknacks and Makonde carvings on Independence Avenue, but nothing worth a pilgrimage, and she does not visit Father's grave. I have never returned. The rancour is still there.

But then I read a poem by the same prairie poet whose Aunt Agnes had cautioned him not to swallow cherry stones, or a cherry tree would sprout out his belly. This same venerated poet wrote that what we banish from our souls is what actually remains. The poem has startled me with a blue sunflower. I had exiled Swahili from my bones. I had taken a new lover, my under-the-rose, my Prairies. But even under the blue bin sky, traces of a stompy orange home exist. A ghost. Even after a banishment of over thirty-five years, Swahili is still my liver.

I acknowledge her presence pole-pole, ever so gently, like candy language, lifting each finger to my lips, licking each one like a Bensons toffee from Father's shop.

And I begin where children usually begin. Counting one-to-ten in Swahili.

Moja, mbili, tatu, nne, tano, sita, saba, nane, tisa.

Kumi.

Acknowledgments

I am very grateful to Robyn Read, my editor at Freehand Books, for her thorough work on the manuscript. Her suggestions, comments, and careful (and provident) reading of the book in its various stages have been invaluable. I am grateful to Sarah Ivany for marketing and promotion, and to the editorial board at Freehand Books for their support of the manuscript. I am grateful to Aritha van Herk for reading an earlier draft, for fur stories, for trips to Millarville Farmers' Market, and for Ian Tyson. I am grateful to Suzette Mayr for reading another version of the manuscript. I am grateful to Larissa Lai for her comments about chong, a Korean sensibility that I explore in the chapter "Away From Home, An Upright Place," which enabled me to push ahead. I am grateful to Sadru Jetha for giving one of the characters in the manuscript the perfect name of Fathlo, and to Sukrita Paul Kumar from whom I learned the phrase "gorh gorh gola," meaning, "a sweet, sweet ball of sugary treat" ("gor gor sweet"). I am grateful to Anne Hanley for her astute gallery eye, Famous Grouse, and introducing me to Margaret Forster's writing. I am grateful to Syama Menon for the beach, coffee, laughter, and printouts. I am grateful to Rashid Al-Hosni for being my running buddy; to Hamdy Al-Shalawy for fish and sunset stories; to Linda Anderson (now retired from the Royal Bank of Canada) who was always there for me; to my apartment in Muscat that lent me silence; and finally, to the cities that have served as my go-betweens, swelling my pleasure, my own love, for Calgary, my Prairies.

Thanking my unnamed.

There is a scene in Elizabeth Hay's *The Only Snow in Havana* in which the narrator, after she has bunked a Canadian winter, watches a singer at a bar in Havana lift her arm. She observes shiny granules of talcum powder in her armpit. She thinks to herself, this is the only snow she will see in Havana. For me, the narrator witnesses her blue sunflower startle, her tryst with home while in faraway Havana. It was this little scene that gave me the idea to pursue the theme of my narrator's trysts with the prairies in faraway places.

Poet Choi Young-mi's fresh and jarring female voice in *At Thirty, the Party Was Over* created quite a stir among young Koreans on the campus of Chonbuk National University in the 1990s. The lines "You walk / The river stays" is my salaam to poet Fred Wah and his generative dialogue with visual artist Bev Tosh in a collaborative installation entitled *Articulations* ("Watch the river from the bridge / – you move, river stays"). The Aunt Agnes that I transported into my novel is from Robert Kroetsch's *The Hornbooks of Rita K*, and I imagine the young boy to be Kroetsch himself. He is also the venerated poet that I refer to at the end of the novel.

Two informative and insightful books that facilitated my research were Dana April Seidenberg's *Mercantile Adventurers: The World of East African Asians, 1750-1985*, about Indian-East African business empires, freedom fighters, and heroes, and Basharat Peer's *Curfewed Night*, about the plight of Kashmiris in modern India.

I also want to thank the named, be they places or people.

First the places: Household and Sundries and Ramson's Cinema in Dodoma; the tea house Stable Rooted Tree and the two bars 3 x 3 and Dandelion in Chonju. The names are: Amal Kara, Mrs. Bhajaj, Kartar Singh, and Koti Kamanga. Their very names enabled my imagination to take off like an airplane; retaining these names became a tribute.

With foreign words, poems, songs, prayer recitations, ginans (hymns), I hung on to the "hue"; I hung on to the "ping" or emotional connection that I had to these verses, and attempted to recreate that for the reader. With Hindi films, instinctively I turned to juggling the aesthetics of 1960s romances with songs from other periods.

The above have been my influencers—my ping.

Early drafts for two small sections of this novel previously appeared in *West Coast Line* Issues 32. 2-3 (Fall/Winter 1998) and 44 38. 2 (Fall 2004) as the articles "And I Will Not Let You Down Like Heer" and "Tender Boon" respectively.

An earlier draft of "Coca-Cola and Cowboys" won the short story competition in the professional category for CBC Radio's *Alberta Anthology* in 2004. It was broadcast on CBC Radio's *Wild Rose Country*, 26 February 2004, and *Daybreak Alberta*, 28 February 2004.

Fragments from the poem "My Hyderabadi Earrings" that appeared in *Open Letter* 9. 3 (Summer 1995) have been embedded into the love notes to the Prairies.

Yasmin Ladha is a Canadian fiction writer, currently working in Muscat, Oman. She completed her BA and MA in the Department of English at the University of Calgary. Her work has appeared in various Canadian journals and anthologies, and she is the author of the collection of short stories *Lion's Granddaughter and Other Stories* (NeWest Press, 1992), the chapbook *Bridal Hands on the Maple* (Second Wednesday Press, 1992), and a book of short stories, documentary-fiction, personal essays, and poetry entitled *Women Dancing on Rooftops: Bring your Belly Close* (TSAR, 1997).

 Recycled
Supporting responsible use
of forest resources
www.fsc.org Cert no. SGS-COC-003153
© 1996 Forest Stewardship Council
FSC   100%

Marquis Book Printing Inc.

Québec, Canada
2010

Printed on Silva Enviro 100% post-consumer EcoLogo certified paper,
processed chlorine free and manufactured using biogas energy.

100%   PERMANENT